THE DEBT

INSTALLMENT ONE

THE DEBT

Installment One: Catch the Zolt

Installment Two: Turn off the Lights

Installment Three: Bring Back Cerberus

Installment Four: Fetch the Treasure Hunter

Installment Five: Yamashita's Gold

Installment Six: Take a Life

THE DEBT

INSTALLMENT ONE

CATCH THE ZOLT

PHILLIP GWYNNE

Kane Miller
A DIVISION OF EDC PUBLISHING

Kane Miller, A Division of EDC Publishing

Cover and text design by Natalie Winter
Cover photography: (boy) by Alan Richardson Photography, model: Nicolai Laptev; (speedboat) by Getty Images

For information contact:
Kane Miller, A Division of EDC Publishing
PO Box 470663
Tulsa, OK 74147-0663

www.kanemiller.com
www.edcpub.com
www.usbornebooksandmore.com

Library of Congress Control Number: 2013953410

Printed and bound in the United States of America
4 5 6 7 8 9 10
ISBN: 978-1-61067-303-7

To Reg,
a good mate gone too soon

THE DAY I TURNED FIFTEEN

My fifteenth birthday started off pretty much like every other day: the alarm on my iPhone going off at 5:30 a.m., playing the song I hated most in the world, "Who Let the Dogs Out." I was forced to get out of bed, stumble across the room and turn off the alarm. Now that I was out of bed, I'd stay out of bed. So, once again, the despicable Baha Men had done their job.

The night before Mom – yes, Mom – had suggested that, because it was my birthday, I should take the day off.

"You're always running," she said. "Enough with the running."

Mom, my mum, is one hundred percent American, one hundred percent Californian. Even though she's been here for more than twenty years she still talks like an American. She calls a footpath a "sidewalk."

She pronounces aluminium “a-*loom*-i-num.” A buoy a “boo-ee.” So that’s why all us kids, and even Dad sometimes, call her Mom and not Mum.

However, my coach Gus – who also happens to be my grandfather – hadn’t agreed with Mom.

Which wasn’t unusual, by the way, because they don’t agree on a lot of things.

He said that I couldn’t really afford to take the day off, not with the Queensland titles less than a month away.

I put on my running gear: singlet, shorts, socks, but not my shoes, and padded down the hall, past my brother’s bedroom, my sister’s bedroom, my parents’ bedroom. As I descended the circular staircase I could hear a noise, which became a news anchor’s voice.

“We interrupt our regular bulletin to bring you this breaking news: it has been reported that sixteen-year-old Otto Zolton-Bander, also known as the Facebook Bandit, a modern-day Robin Hood, has been captured.”

Somebody must’ve left the television on last night.

But as I reached the ground floor I could see Dad, still in his pajamas, remote in his hand, intent on the plasma screen.

Mom always jokes that if Dad ever gets sick of being a business tycoon he could get a job on TV as a presenter on one of those lifestyle programs. Not that he would ever do that, but I know exactly what she means: he has that sort of wholesome, easy-on-the-eye look about him.

"Dad!" I said. "What are you doing up this early?"

"Happy birthday to you," he sang, giving it the full Pavarotti. "Happy birthday to you. Happy birthday, dear Dominic. Happy birthday to you!"

"That really was tremendous, Dad," I said. "But I wouldn't give up my day job if I were you."

Not that I really have any idea what his day job is.

"And we're still on for tonight?" he said. "Your grandfather's after your birthday dinner?"

There wasn't going to be a big party for my birthday this year as Mom and I had decided that we'd save that for next year, for my sixteenth.

"Secret men's business?" I said, smiling.

"Secret men's business," he repeated, not smiling.

"Sure," I said.

Dad flashed his TV-presenter smile, before turning his attention back to the screen.

I said good-bye and kept walking.

Sitting on the front steps, I put on my running shoes, lacing them up tight, strapped the heart monitor around my chest, set the timer and took off.

It was one of those warm, cloudless days that are typical of the Gold Coast. Even more typical of Halcyon Grove, the gated community where we live. According to the Halcyon Grove Country Club, we have twenty-seven more golf-friendly days than

any other place in the country. Not that my parents ever take advantage of that, because they are always too busy: my father making money and my mother giving that money away. But I think they like the fact that if they ever do decide to take a day off to play a round of golf, they'll have had twenty-seven more to choose from.

There are no fences within Halcyon Grove and each house is like an ocean liner – white, gleaming, multistoried – afloat on a sea of green. At this time of the morning the only people on the streets were the workers going to work: the nannies, the gardeners, the canine-fitness facilitators. They hurried past me, heads down, avoiding eye contact. As I ran past the Havillands' house I did what I always do: looked up at the second story.

Imogen was there, as usual, her face framed by the window.

Once she and I were at Robina Mall when a total stranger, a man with a phony tan in a linen suit, came up and offered to turn her into the world's next supermodel. At first I thought he was some sort of perve – there's no shortage of those at Robina Mall – or that he was joking – Imogen a super-freaking-model? But he was serious. He gave her a glossy business card, told her to discuss it with her parents and then call him when "she was ready."

When I looked up at the window I tried to imagine

Imogen as a supermodel, Imogen strutting down a catwalk in Paris or Milan. But I couldn't. All I could see was the Imogen I'd known my whole life.

She held up a piece of paper, on which was printed **Happy Birthday Dipstick**. Even from here I recognized the font as Gotham, and I felt sort of honored that she'd called me a dipstick in her favorite typeface.

I smiled up at her, but as I did my foot clipped something – the wheel of a bicycle – and I stumbled, just managing to regain my balance and stop myself from sprawling to the ground.

"Idiot!" I yelled, thinking how catastrophic a sprained ankle would've been this close to my race.

Maybe his little sister had left it there accidentally but I couldn't help thinking that Tristan Jazy had done it on purpose. I looked up at the Jazys' house, half expecting to see him there, watching from a window, that trademark smirk on his face. But all the windows – and there were a lot of them – had their blinds down.

Rap is crap, sharks are cool, under no circumstances should dads ever be allowed to wear Speedos, and Tristan Jazy was so not okay!

It took me five minutes and thirty-two and a half seconds to get to the gate. I had my usual brief conversation with Samsoni, the Tongan guard, as I ran slowly through the pedestrian entrance.

"You're better off running inside, Mr. Silvagni," he said.

I wish he wouldn't call me Mr. Silvagni. I wish he'd call me "Dom." Or "kid." Or even "bro." But it's one of the rules of the Halcyon Grove Body Corporate: *At all times Employees are to address Residents with the appropriate honorific.*

"No topographical variation inside, Samsoni," I said, which is what I always said.

And Samsoni gave the same resigned smile he always gives. He, like me, knows that runners, especially middle distance runners, need topographical variation.

I followed the Halcyon Grove wall around, turning into a small street. Its official name is Byron Street, but because it's lined with trees, and the trees are full of birds, who at this time of the morning were in full chirp, I'd renamed it Chirp Street. And Chirp Street was where I encountered my first topographical variation. It wasn't really a hill, more of a bump, but it was still a chance to increase my heart rate without increasing my pace.

Chirp Street is never a busy street, especially so early, and I was surprised when out of the corner of my eye I noticed a white van approaching from behind. Cars – or vans – aren't really my thing and I couldn't have told you what make it was. I was pretty sure I hadn't seen one like this before, though.

It was streamlined, sort of futuristic-looking, and seemed to be making no noise at all. And because the sun was glinting off the windshield, I couldn't make out who was driving.

The van was about three meters behind me, moving at the same speed I was. When I sped up, so did the van. When I slowed down, so did the van. I thought of Samsoni's mantra: *You're better off running inside, Mr. Silvagni*, and how I'd always dismissed it.

Yes, this kid from my school, Jason Walker, had been kidnapped a couple of years ago. Yes, they'd cut off his left ear. Yes, his parents had paid a million dollars to get him – or the remainder of him – back, but I'd always thought that was because he was a soft target, exactly the sort of dorky rich kid a kidnapper would kidnap. That couldn't possibly happen to me, I'd thought. But here I was, on a deserted street, with an ominous-looking van following me. Maybe there was an innocent explanation for its presence, but it was the less innocent ones that were competing for my attention.

As the van got closer, my brain started whirring, making that noise that a hard disk makes when you dump a load of data on it.

What to do next?

Suddenly, a *swoosh!* sound, and then blackness. Just like when I'd had my appendix out a few years ago and had been "put to sleep" by the anesthetist.

When I regained consciousness, I was lying on the footpath.

Out of the corner of my eye I could see the white van disappearing around a corner.

I did a quick inventory, wriggling each limb in turn. It didn't feel as if there was anything broken. I couldn't see any obvious abrasions.

Okay, so the van hadn't hit me, I thought, as I carefully got to my feet.

But what had happened to me?

And then I noticed it: a small red lump on the back of my right hand. I ran my fingers across it. It was like I'd been stung by a wasp or a bee.

So maybe I had been anesthetized, and this was where the needle, or whatever they'd used, had gone in.

In that case, I should call the police.

I even took my iPhone out to do just that.

But then I had second thoughts: what, exactly, was I going to tell the cops? And what, exactly, would they do?

Above me the sun was shining in the cloud-free sky. Around me the birds were chirping.

I put my iPhone back into my pocket.

This was weird, but it was my birthday and I wasn't going to let this spoil it.

So I did what I always did: I ran. And when I was running, really running, concentrating on form, pace, rhythm, there wasn't much room or anything else in my brain; I immediately stopped thinking about what had happened.

I took the bridge across the canal and entered the next suburb, Chevron Heights. After sleepy Halcyon Grove, Chevron Heights was always a bit of a shock. Even this early it was busy: shopkeepers were readying their shops for the day's business, people were waiting at bus stops. Some workers were putting the finishing touches on yet another new office for Coast Home Loans; it seemed like every corner on the coast had one now.

Up ahead I could see the diminutive figure of Seb, waiting for me, as usual, just outside Big Pete's Pizzas, running up and down on the spot.

Seb is half a head shorter than me, quite a few kilos lighter – he's a bit of a runt. In most sports this would be a disadvantage – bit-of-a-runt basketballers don't slam dunk; who wants to watch a bit-of-a-runt footballer? Not middle distance running, however. The last three 1500 meters world record holders – Saïd Aouita, Noureddine Morceli, Hicham El Guerrouj – have each been a bit of a runt. I used to be a bit of a runt too. But this season I've shot up. Bulked up. And even though I'm still ranked first in my school in both the 800 meters and the 1500 meters, my lack of runtiness was starting to worry me.

Long black hair tied back, knee-length basketball shorts, sleeveless T-shirt – Seb looked more like a skater than a runner. And maybe he is a skater – how would I know? – but he's definitely a runner, and a pretty good one. That's how we first met. Earlier this year we kept crossing paths – literally – on our respective early-morning runs. Initially we just acknowledged each other, then we started talking and then we started running together.

"You're late," said Seb.

"No, I'm not," I said.

"Yes, you are."

If I left at the usual time – which I had – and ran at the usual pace – which I had – then I'd arrive at Big Pete's at 6:12. When I checked my watch it said *6:16*. Seb was right: I'd lost four minutes.

I didn't have time to ponder this further because we'd reached the start of the biggest climb on our regular run, the topographical variation we call the Gut Buster. As I was coming up to a big race, I was in a taper, which meant that I shouldn't push it, that I should "apply the hand brake" as Gus said. Seb wasn't in a taper, which meant that he could do what he liked, run as hard as he wanted to.

Keep that hand brake on, I told myself as Seb moved ahead of me, opening up a two-meter lead.

You need to conserve energy, I told myself as the lead stretched to five meters.

Are you really going to let this runt beat you to the top? I asked myself as I released the hand brake and powered up the hill, passing Seb just before the crest.

Immediately I knew that my heart rate was higher than it should be, that Gus would see this when he downloaded the data from my heart monitor, that he probably wouldn't be happy. This was exactly why he always insisted I didn't train with anybody, and why I hadn't told him anything about Seb.

Cruising down the hill towards the rising sun, the sea breeze in our faces, we continued on the rest of our regular loop, running along the side of the Ibbotson Reserve.

That's its official name but we all call it Preacher's Forest on account of this mad old man, the Preacher, who's been camping there forever.

It's a huge tract of land – parts of which are rain forest, parts of which are mangroves, parts of which are sand hills – with creeks running through it, a large swampy lake in the middle and a disused airfield on the other side. Every second week there's a developer on the news talking about how the future of the Gold Coast depends on Ibbotson Reserve being developed. Followed by a conservationist talking about how the future of the Gold Coast depends on Ibbotson Reserve not being developed.

We could hear the Preacher's voice, indulging in one of his customary rants.

"Doomed to destruction, happy is he who repays you for what you have done to us!"

Seb and I exchanged looks: what a crazy old bugger!

"Doomed to destruction!" repeated Seb.

Thirty-two minutes later and we were approaching Big Pete's from the other direction. When we passed Big Pete's, Seb said, "Loose as a goose on the juice," before disappearing down a side street, headed for wherever it was he headed for when he left me.

I've never been to Seb's house. I've never met his family. I'm not even sure what school he goes to. If he even goes to school. And when I googled his name, or the name he'd told me – Sebastian Baresi – all that came up was the bass player in this Italian death metal band called Del Diavolo Testicoli. Really, all I know about Seb is that he loved running.

As I crossed the bridge again Elliott the kelpie joined me, barking, wagging his tail. I didn't know whose dog he was – I'd named him after Herb Elliott, the champion Australian runner of the fifties – but every morning, at the same place, he joined me.

"Good boy, Elliott!" I said.

Just as we were about to enter Chirp Street, Elliott left me, as he always did.

"Bye, Elliott!" I said, and he responded with one of his staccato barks.

All the way back home I had this feeling that somebody was watching me, monitoring me.

It had been a strange morning. A really strange morning. But, hey, maybe this was what life was all about when you were fifteen years old.

SECRET MEN'S BUSINESS

A lamp on top of the desk threw out a weak light, leaving pockets of darkness in Gus's office. I couldn't even see the floor-to-ceiling bookshelves, let alone read the titles of its many books, but I knew that mostly they were about running. The other walls were covered in framed photos, posters and newspaper clippings, also to do with running. Somewhere in the shadows Roger Bannister was breaking the four-minute mile, John Landy was setting the 1500 meters world record in 1954, and Hicham El Guerrouj was setting the current world record of three minutes and twenty-six seconds.

Dad and Gus were sitting beside each other on one of the two leather couches, I was on the other. My mum had discarded those couches about fifty annoying redecorations and eighty even more annoying decorators ago. Yes, the leather is cracked and, yes, the cushions are lumpy, but those couches are just the thing – or “just the ticket,” as Gus would say – for stretching out and reading the latest edition of *Running World.*

Gus was wearing his usual clothes: a faded tank top that showed off his ropy old-man muscles, and shorts that were baggy, but not baggy enough to hide the stump. When Gus first arrived at Halcyon Grove I was terrified of the stump. But then I got used to “Stumpy” with his funny little seamed head. Like an eyeless alien from a C-grade sci-fi movie. Even so, I preferred it when Gus wore his prosthetic, but I guess when you’ve been strapping an artificial leg on since you were fifteen years old, you’re going to get pretty sick of it.

Dad and Gus were drinking whisky – straight, on the rocks – from hefty tumblers, and I had a glass of Coke. In the last few minutes the wind had picked up outside and occasionally, from the empty top floor of Gus’s house, came the sound of a branch rapping on a window with its wooden knuckles.

Dad and Gus kept exchanging looks, clearing their throats, as if neither knew exactly how to start this conversation. So I did it for them, saving them some pretty major embarrassment.

“I know all about sex,” I told them. “We did it at school.”

"You did it?" Dad asked.

"Yeah, last term. With Mrs. Prefontaine."

"Mrs. Prefontaine?"

"Yes, she taught us all about it. Well, the basics anyway."

A look of relief crossed Dad's smooth face.

"Dom, we didn't actually want to talk to you about the birds and the bees," he said.

"The birds and the bees?"

"Your father means sex," said Gus.

"There's something much more serious we need to discuss," said Dad.

"I thought sex was really serious," I said. "Mrs. Prefontaine seemed to think it was, anyway."

Gus took over again, putting on his "me coach, you athlete" voice.

"You know what a debt is, don't you, Dom?"

That's a pretty dumb question, I thought. *I might be an athlete but I ain't stupid.*

"Yes, I'm familiar with the concept."

Gus looked over at Dad before he said, "Well, our family has a debt."

"An enormous debt," added Dad.

"You mean money?" I asked, thinking of the house we live in; this house, which my parents had bought for Gus; our beach house at Byron Bay; all Mom's jewelry.

"No, not money. Another sort of debt."

Now my brain was doing some work: what other sorts of debt were there?

Suddenly it occurred to me that this might be an elaborate practical joke, played on all male Silvagnis when they reach the age of fifteen. I scanned the room, looking for hidden cameras. But I couldn't see any. And let's face it, neither Dad nor Gus are the practical-joking types.

Gus got up, moved to his desk, took a key from somewhere and unlocked the bottom right drawer. I'd always wondered why that drawer was locked, what it was Gus wanted to keep secret from me. He slid it open and brought out an old-fashioned binder with an embossed cover, the leather red and worn. He brought it back over to the couch, sat down, took a gulp of his whisky. Carefully opening the binder, Gus took a photo from inside and leaned forward to hand it to me.

"You know who this is?" he said.

"Of course," I said, looking at the bearded man in the hat and the cape in the sepia-toned photo. "I was named after him. He's Dominic, my great-great-great-great-grandfather."

"That's right," said Gus smiling at me. "My great-great-grandfather."

"And my great-great-great-grandfather," said Dad.

"So what do you know about him?" said Gus.

"Let's see," I said. "That he was destined for greatness?"

Okay, it probably wasn't the best joke I'd ever come up with but it deserved some sort of acknowledgement: a smile at least, but I got nothing from Gus and Dad.

Actually, I knew a lot about Dominic Silvagni because last year, when we had to do a school project about one of our ancestors, I chose him. Probably because he was the only one I could find a photo of. According to Gus there'd been a fire in his old house that had destroyed a whole lot of family photos.

"He was born in Italy, in Calabria, in a village called San Luca in 1822. In 1851 he married Maria Barassi. They came to Australia during the Gold Rush in 1852. He was killed in the Eureka Stockade in 1854, which was a rebellion by miners against the heavy taxation imposed on them by the Victorian government. A month after his death his son, my great-great-great-grandfather, was born," I said.

I remembered how proud I'd been at school to read out my namesake's history. Especially when Mr. Ryan said that the men who had died at Eureka Stockade were heroes, that they'd stood up for their rights, that they'd helped form the democratic nation of Australia.

"That's very good," said Gus. "But there's one more thing you need to know."

He drank some more whisky, then opened his mouth as if to talk, but no words came out.

"Dominic Silvagni was born into a 'Ndrangheta family," said Dad.

"He was what?" I said.

"Pen and paper?" said Dad to Gus.

My grandfather stomped over to his desk, returning with a pad and a black felt-tip pen. Dad opened the pad to a blank page and wrote in capital letters: *'NDRANGHETA*.

Written down, it looked sort of familiar.

"Isn't it like the Mafia or something?" I said.

"Like the Mafia, but not as nice," said Dad.

At first I thought he was joking, but there was not a trace of humor in his face.

Gus, who seemed to have found his voice again, proceeded to explain the origins of the 'Ndrangheta.

Apparently in ancient Italy it was an organization formed by peasant farmers to fight against the injustices of rich landlords. But over time it evolved into a criminal enterprise.

"So if he was a member of the 'Ndrangheta," I said, stumbling over the pronunciation, "why did he come to Australia?"

Again Dad and Gus looked at each other.

"Because he wanted out," said Dad.

"Out of the 'Ndrangheta?"

Dad nodded.

"Usually that's not possible, because if you're born into a 'Ndrangheta family then you are a 'Ndranghetista for life, but somehow he persuaded them to accept a sum of money in return for his, well, freedom."

"How much money?"

"The modern-day equivalent would be around two million dollars," said Dad.

I emitted a low whistle. "How did he get that much?"

"He didn't," said Dad, and there was no mistaking the contempt in his voice.

"He would've!" said Gus. "If he hadn't given his life."

"Given his life?" said Dad mockingly. "He died like a dog for a cause that had nothing to do with him."

Although I hadn't heard it before, this sounded like an old argument, one in which the same phrases came from the same mouths over and over again.

Dad continued. "Your great-great-great-great-grandfather came to Australia to prospect for gold, to find his fortune and pay back this debt. But then he went and got himself killed."

"For a cause he believed –" started Gus, before Dad interjected, "Dad, just show it to your grandson."

Gus took a plastic sleeve out of the folder. Within it was a document, ancient-looking, the paper yellowed, brittle.

"The 'Ndrangheta weren't about to let Dominic just take off to the other side of the world, never to hear from him again," explained Dad. "So before he left they made him sign this."

"Be very careful," said Gus, handing it to me.

I took the paper from him. It was titled *Pagherò Cambiario.*

"But it's in Italian," I said.

"Basically it's a debt agreement," said Dad. "It says that if the loan is defaulted, which is what happened, then all male Silvagnis, upon reaching the age of fifteen, must make six repayments on this debt."

"Repayments?" I said. "Money?"

"No, not money. Think of them more like assignments."

This was getting too weird; I had to close my eyes. The 'Ndrangheta, defaulted loans, assignments: what the blazes was going on?

When I opened my eyes again I wanted it to all go away. Or Dad and Gus to be laughing because of the great joke they'd just played on me.

Slowly, I opened my eyes.

They weren't laughing. It was no joke.

"What sort of assignments?" I said.

"They will let you know," said Dad.

"They? The 'Ndrangheta, you mean?"

"It's probably better you don't use that word," said Dad, tearing the piece of paper out of the pad and scrunching it up. "Just think of them as The Debt."

Suddenly I was reminded of the van, white, streamlined, futuristic-looking, the missing four minutes.

"They've already contacted you?" said Dad, studying my face.

"I think so," I said, and I told them what had happened.

"So there were no injuries or anything?" asked Gus.

"Not really," I said, but then I remembered. "There was, like, this red lump on the back of my right hand."

I pointed to where it had been, and Gus gently ran his fingers across the surface of my skin.

"And now I have this, like, weird feeling that I'm being –" I started, but Dad held up both hands as if to say *Stop*.

"We don't want to know, okay? We can't know. It's between you and The Debt."

I looked across at Gus. He had a resigned look on his face as if to say *I'm afraid your dad's right on this.*

"Okay, what if I refuse to make these installments, to do these assignments?" I said. "What can they possibly do to me?"

"In caso du mancato pagamento, il crediture può riclamane una libbra della carne del debitore," Gus read from the document.

"What in blazes does that mean?"

"In the event of the debtor defaulting on his repayments the creditor is entitled to take a pound of flesh."

"A pound of flesh?" I said.

"That's right," said Dad.

The expression was familiar – wasn't it from Shakespeare or something? – but what exactly did it mean in this context? My eyes were drawn towards Gus. And his crutches. And his stump.

No, it can't be.

"Your leg?" I asked.

Gus nodded.

"It wasn't cancer?"

Gus shook his head. "There was no cancer."

"You didn't repay The Debt?"

Gus nodded.

"And that's what they did to you?" I asked, pointing.

"They took their pound of flesh," said Gus.

This answer, literally, took my breath away. Struggling for air, I slumped onto the couch.

Again I had that feeling that this wasn't happening, this wasn't real.

But when I looked up at the walls, I could see the

same appalled look on the shadowed faces of Roger Bannister, John Landy, Hicham El Guerrouj, all the runners assembled there.

The Debt took their pound of flesh!

As I looked at my dad, in his immaculate short-sleeved shirt and his immaculate chinos, something occurred to me.

"And you did repay The Debt?"

"I did what I had to do," he replied, throwing Gus a look of utter scorn. "I dragged our family back out of the sewer."

What was going on here? I knew that there hadn't been a lot of money around when Dad was growing up but I'd never heard him describe it as a "sewer" before.

"But why would Dominic sign such a thing?" I said.

"You've got to remember," said Gus, "they were very different, shall we say unenlightened, times. Red in tooth and claw. And your great-great-great-great-grandfather was an optimist. He was certain he would make that money, that he would dig that much gold out of the ground."

"The man was a fool," said Dad.

Gus's grip on his whisky tumbler tightened.

"A fool who bred fools," continued Dad in a tone of voice – sneering, dismissive – I'd not heard him use before. "Or if you want to put it in more modern terms, the fool gene has had a big say in our family history."

Gus's knuckles were white, the ice clinking as the glass shook.

"But we're breeding it out, and that's the main thing," said Dad.

He looked at me and smiled.

"Isn't that right, Dom?"

There was a loud knocking sound from upstairs.

I knew, logically, that it must've been that branch rapping on the windowpane. But right then it seemed to be something else, a herald, because something very dark and very sinister had just come into my life.

Dad sloshed the last of the whisky into his and Gus's glasses and said, "There's just one more thing, Dom."

"For heaven's sake, David!" said Gus.

My dad glared at his dad, jabbed his finger at the document and said, "It's The Debt!"

Gus sat with his head bowed for a while before he seemed to gather himself, got up from the couch and went back over to the open drawer of his desk. When he returned he had something in his hand. It had a wooden handle, an embossed tip.

Was it a sort of stamp?

"Okay," said Dad. "Let's get this over and done with."

Both he and Gus undid their belts and lowered their pants. Dad pointed to high up on the inside of his right thigh. Within a rectangle, there was a single word: *PAGATO*. At first I thought that it was some sort of tattoo, but then I realized that it was formed from scarred flesh not inked flesh, that it was a brand.

I wondered why I hadn't ever seen it before. But when I thought about it, Dad had never been a walk-around-stark-naked sort of dad; he always wore board shorts when he went swimming, never a Speedo. I looked over at Gus, leaning on his crutch. I could see that he had the same brand, and it was in the same place.

Or was it the same?

His brand was less distinct than Dad's and it was harder to read, but it seemed to be incomplete somehow.

"The mark of the debtor," said Dad.

Now I knew that it was a branding iron, not a stamp.

"No!" I said, getting to my feet.

My fight-or-flight response had kicked in, and it was getting ready to get me out of there.

Gus put his hand around my wrist.

It was a strange gesture and not something that he'd done before.

But I immediately knew what he was saying: *there's no escaping this, Dom. But I'm here to look after you.*

As I looked into his face, into his old-man eyes,

I realized that I trusted Gus more than I trusted anybody else in the world.

I let myself fall back onto the couch.

Dad took an antique Zippo lighter from the desk's drawer.

His thumb came down and a huge flame leapt up.

"Whoa!" I said.

"Don't make them like this anymore," said Dad.

"Drink this," said Gus, handing me his glass of whisky as Dad heated the tip of the branding iron. I swallowed it in one gulp. The liquid slid down my throat, and then exploded, a fireball in my guts.

"Whoa!" I repeated.

"You ready?" said Dad.

No, of course I'm not ready. This is ridiculous. This is crazy. But when I looked over at my father and my grandfather, the two men in the world who loved me the most, I knew I had to trust them.

"Yes," I said, pulling down my jeans and baring the inside of my right thigh.

Dad brought the tip of the branding iron closer and I could feel the heat, feel the hairs singeing.

I couldn't help it, I moved my leg away.

"You need Gus to hold your leg?" said Dad.

"No!" I said.

Instead I held out my hand for Gus to hold.

"I love you, Dom," Dad said, his voice low and reassuring.

"I love you too, Dad."

I tensed my leg, and he pressed the branding iron firmly into my skin. The pain was indescribable, like nothing I'd felt before, like nothing I'd ever want to feel again. I squeezed Gus's hand so tight, it's a wonder I didn't break his fingers. But almost worse than the pain was the smell, the nauseating smell of my own searing flesh.

It seemed like minutes, it was probably seconds, but eventually Dad said, "Son, it's done."

Despite the pain, despite the smell, a thought occurred to me: *We've all got the same mark now.*

I looked down at my thigh expecting to see the same brand as Dad's, but instead there was just an empty rectangle, red and raw.

It took me a while to think this through, but when I did I let out an almost involuntary, "No!"

I would be branded after each successful installment. Which is why Dad's brand was complete and Gus's wasn't.

So even if I did repay an installment, it would be with the knowledge that this indescribable pain would follow.

"No!" I said, as I charged at Dad, fists raised high.

How could my own father let this happen to me?

I wanted to pummel him, crack every bone in his body.

But Dad wrapped me in a bear hug.

"No!" I kept repeating, struggling to get free. But it was no use, he was much stronger than he looked.

Finally there were no more "no"s and I let myself go limp.

Dad released me and when I stepped away I could see the wet patch my hot tears had made on his shirt.

He and I walked back home, not talking.

But as I was about to disappear into my bedroom, he said, "Dom, whatever you do, don't mess with The Debt."

I said nothing.

"Okay, Dom?" he said, hands gripping my shoulders, his eyes searching mine.

"Okay, Dad," I said.

YOU DON'T MESS WITH THE DEBT

At five thirty the following morning, when the appalling Baha Men expressed their usual concern regarding the dogs and their escape, I felt relieved.

I'd been awake all night.

With the inside of my thigh aching, thoughts ricocheting around inside my head, there'd been no chance of sleep. But now, at last, I had the excuse I needed to get out of bed. I was lathered with sweat and my sheets were twisted into a knot as tight as the one Imogen used to put in her hair when her mother let her go to ballet lessons.

As I got ready for my morning run, as I went through the ritual of padding barefoot down the hall, of lacing up my shoes on the outside step, I started to feel better.

When I started running, however, the brand began to ache again.

But when I passed the Havilland house and saw that Imogen was there as usual, I couldn't help but smile. My family, apparently, had a debt, The Debt; I had a brand burned onto my thigh; my life had changed – but this, Imogen standing at the window, was the same.

She scribbled on the windowpane with an imaginary pencil. *Have you finished your math assignment?*

I shook my head. *No*

She pointed at herself. *Do you want me to help*? I replied with a thumbs-up. *I sure do.*

Chirp Street was its usual chirpy self and Seb was outside Big Pete's, running up and down on the spot, ponytail flicking from one shoulder to the other.

As we cruised down the Gut Buster a police car roared past, lights flashing, siren blaring.

Last night Dad and Gus had been so adamant, so obstinate: no police! *Omertà*, they'd called it. Code of silence. This matter has nothing to do with the police, they'd said. In that half-lit office, the atmosphere thick and fetid with conspiracy, I'd had no choice but to agree with them. But now, the breeze bringing the tang of the sea, sunlight splashing on my face, I realized how wrong that was. Nobody had the right to take the leg of any fifteen-year-old kid, especially not a runner! It was

morally wrong. It was legally wrong. It was wrong, wrong, wrong.

I'll contact the police. I'll put an end to this.

But as I made this resolution I had that feeling again: somebody was watching me.

"It was your birthday yesterday, right?" Seb said as we approached Big Pete's.

"How did you know that?" I said, because I couldn't remember ever telling him.

Seb hesitated for a second before he said, "Hey, it was on the net, right? Not possible to keep your birthday a secret anymore."

On the net? Okay, maybe it was on Facebook, but Seb wasn't my Facebook friend.

"So you're fifteen now, right?" said Seb.

I nodded.

"Then you're three days older than me."

"Your birthday's on Tuesday?"

"Sure is."

"But you're still okay for the race?"

"Absolutely."

Getting Seb involved with the school track team hadn't exactly been easy to organize. If I'd have told the football coach that I knew this kid who was a whiz-bang footballer, he'd have been down to Seb's place – wherever that was – in a second, a scholarship application in his hands. But middle distance running, unlike football, or cricket or even surfing, isn't a sexy sport. Not in my school. Not in my state. Not in my country.

It was the video I'd taken with my iPhone of Seb running that had done the job, however. Coach Sheeds had taken one look at that, at Seb's loose, easy style and had agreed: this kid deserved a shot.

"It's some sort of qualification race, isn't it?" said Seb.

"Technically," I said. "But it's also a big chance for you to show Coach Sheeds what you've got."

Unfortunately, because Seb wasn't a student at the school, he couldn't compete for us. Not yet, not until he was on a scholarship.

"Cool," said Seb. "I'll be there."

"Great," I said.

He gave me a "Loose as a goose on the juice" before he ran off.

Now, I told myself. *Now is the time to do it.* I ran back up the street, turning right at the new Coast Home Loans office. Past my old primary school and I was there. I hesitated before I went inside. Again there was that feeling that I was being watched, that I was being monitored.

No, it had to be done, I told myself.

Up the steps, through the door and I was in the police station.

An older cop with a pot belly glanced up at me when I entered, but immediately looked back down again.

"Excuse me?" I said.

"Yes," he said, a note of annoyance in his voice. "How can I help you today?"

Now I wished I hadn't been so impetuous and had spent some time rehearsing what I was going to say.

My own father had mutilated me with a branding iron? Yeah, right.

They'd threatened to amputate my leg. As if.

"Can I help you, son?" said Pot Belly. "It might not look like it, but I've got a lot of work to get through today."

"Actually, not right now," I said, and I turned around and walked out.

I had to figure out what to say. I'd come back later in the day when I had it right.

I ran back down the street, back past Coast Home Loans.

After I'd crossed the bridge again, Elliott joined me. He was his usual noisy tail-wagging self and that morning I was especially glad to see him. I even told him this.

"Elliott, it's so good to see you!"

When you run all the time on the streets like me, like Seb, like Elliott, you develop what Gus calls a "runner's sixth sense" about traffic.

We came to a crossroad. My eyes hadn't seen a car, my ears hadn't heard any traffic, my nose hadn't smelled any traffic and my body hadn't felt the vibration of traffic. There was no traffic, so there was no need to break stride as I moved from the footpath onto the road.

I was halfway across the road, Elliott just behind me, and there was still no sound, no smell, no vibration. But then there was a black motorbike, with a rider clad all in black, headed straight for us. I jumped out of the way. The motorbike missed me, its back wheel brushing my leg. But it collected Elliott, catapulting him skyward.

In slo-mo I watched him fall, dog-paddling in the air, his black-and-tan fur twisting against the blue of the golf-friendly sky. Watched him hit the road with a thud.

He didn't move.

I hurried towards him.

"Elliott! You okay? Elliott!"

He looked at me, his eyes brown and liquid. He whimpered. And then he died.

"Is everything okay?" came a voice from behind.

I turned to see a man, dressed for jogging, a concerned look on his face.

"Is it your dog?" he said. "Do you want me to do something? Call the police?"

"Not my dog," I said, getting to my feet. "I just found him like this. No need to call the police."

Before he could say anything else, I sprinted off, and the brand on the inside of my thigh started burning anew.

I knew then that I wouldn't be going back to the police station. Not today. Not ever.

SNAP! CRACKLE! POP! UGALI!

Two days later after my morning run I was at my grandfather's house.

"You okay, tiger?" Gus asked, his eyes full of concern as they searched my face.

The words popped into my head: *I'm not a tiger and I'm not okay*.

But that's where they stayed.

"Yeah, I'm okay," I said instead.

But I couldn't stop thinking of poor little Elliott. His furry body dead on the pavement became another not-so-furry body: it became me.

As I ate the breakfast Gus had prepared, he downloaded that morning's data from my heart monitor onto his iMac. Gus is pretty techno savvy. I wouldn't exactly call him a nerd or a geek, but he's definitely not one of those old guys who peck about on a keyboard like a myopic chicken. And if

he doesn't know something, he isn't afraid to ask. Though, usually it's my sister Miranda he directs his questions to.

I dipped my spoon into the bowl of steaming ugali.

"Of what?" you say, and I don't blame you.

As far as breakfast cereals go, ugali isn't really up there. Snap. Crackle. Pop. Ugali! Doesn't happen. Just like a chocolate milkshake, only crunchy. Not quite.

Actually ugali is pretty bland. I reckon that's what ugali means: lumpy stuff with very little flavor. But ugali is what Kenyans eat and, as everybody knows, the Kenyans are incredible middle distance runners. Therefore, if I eat ugali, and lots of it, I'll run fast too.

That's Gus's theory anyway, and I never question Gus's theories because if it hadn't been for him, I wouldn't have become a competitive runner in the first place.

"Dom, stop running!"

If my parents said that to me once when I was a little kid, they said it a million times.

"Dom, please walk!"

But I couldn't help myself. Why walk when you can run? Why go slow when you can go fast?

When I got to school the teachers took over.

"Dom, stop running!"

"Dom, please walk!"

But I couldn't help myself.

In the end my parents took me to a doctor and she gave me these pills, these anti-running pills. They worked, too. I stopped running around and I just sat in the classroom and watched the goldfish being goldfish in the goldfish bowl.

Then Gus came to live next door, with his running books, and his running magazines, and John Landy and Roger Bannister and Hicham El Guerrouj and all those other great runners all over his walls.

"I'm actually a pretty fast runner," I told him one day, but I could tell he didn't believe me.

So for three days I didn't take the anti-running pills, flushing them down the toilet instead, and I went over to Gus's house and told him to come outside and watch me. He watched as I ran around, faster and faster and faster. Then he believed me. I stopped taking the pills for good, Gus became my coach and I became a middle distance runner.

And with all the regular running I did, I no longer felt the need to run around the classroom anymore.

As I ate the ugali, I read last month's edition of *Running World*, an article about the rivalry between Sebastian Coe and Steve Ovett, the great English runners of the eighties. In a ten-day period they traded the mile world record three times!

"How big was Sebastian Coe?" I asked Gus, my mouth full of ugali.

"A hundred and seventy-five centimeters, fifty-four kilos," he replied, demonstrating his customary encyclopedic knowledge of all things to do with middle distance running.

Great, another runt.

"And Steve Ovett?"

"He was a bigger man. A hundred and eighty-three centimeters, seventy kilos."

Immediately, I preferred Steve Ovett. Felt angry because Coe beat him in the 1500 meters final at the 1980 Moscow Olympics.

"Let's see what the weather's doing," said Gus, switching on the TV.

Again they were talking about Otto Zolton-Bander.

Even though everybody knew the Zolt's story, everybody around my age anyway, they were going through it yet again. During the last two years the six-foot-tall juvenile delinquent had broken into many of the luxurious vacation homes on an exclusive part of Reverie Island and stolen goods worth thousands of dollars.

Otto Zolton-Bander had also stolen people's cars, their boats, and, despite never having taken a flying lesson in his life, four different light planes. He'd landed them, too. Well, crash-landed them. But each time he'd walked away unscathed.

As for the Robin Hood bit, somebody who worked

at an animal refuge on the island had let on that they regularly received cash donations from somebody who called themselves "the Zolt."

Apparently a private investigator by the unlikely name of Hound de Villiers had tracked the Zolt down and made a citizen's arrest. The reporter explained that Schedule 1 to the *Criminal Code Act 1899* stated that "it is lawful for any person who believes on reasonable ground that another person has committed the offense to arrest that person without warrant." They showed a photo taken on Hound de Villiers's phone of the Zolt handcuffed to a tree, his knees up around his ears. He was giving the camera a cheesy smile. I couldn't help admiring the Zolt. Imagine smiling like that when you were as handcuffed as that. The story ended with the reporter saying that Hound de Villiers would be bringing the Zolt in to the authorities tomorrow afternoon.

Then it was the weather – the long-range forecast for the next two weeks was fine and hot.

"Promising," said Gus, turning off the TV.

Promising, because I ran well when it was hot. My PB – my personal best – for the 1500 was set when it was thirty-four degrees Celsius.

Gus reckoned it was all the ugali I was eating, that although I was white on the outside, inside I was a heat-loving Kenyan.

"How did they do it?" I asked.

I could tell from the look on Gus's face that he immediately knew what I was talking about.

"We really need to keep our minds on this race, Dom. That's the ticket."

"How did they do it?" I said, pushing away the bowl of ugali.

Gus looked at me, then propped himself on a stool. When he did this, Stumpy poked his head upwards, sort of like one of those meerkats at the zoo, popping out of its burrow.

"If I tell you, will you get your mind back on the race?"

I nodded.

Gus sighed deeply and started the story.

"I've just finished my morning run. The same as you do, but I always used to end with a dip in the ocean. Salt water is isotonic, you know."

I glared at Gus; I wasn't in the mood for one of his customary digressions.

"What happened?" I demanded.

"It's winter, and I'm the only one in the sea. The water's calm, no surf at all. I'm not even swimming, just walking along the bottom. That sort of resistance work is –"

Again, I gave Gus the "no digressions" glare.

"I'm waist deep in the water, it's a beautiful day, and then next thing I know I'm waking up in the hospital."

I interrupted, “But what happened at the beach?”

“I don’t know what happened at the beach. Like I said, one second I’m walking in the water, the next second I’m waking up in the hospital. And there’s all these people looking at me. It takes me a while to realize that they’re doctors. I start to panic, of course. ‘Am I okay?’ I ask. But the head doctor, a man with a lovely smile, says, ‘You’re a very lucky young man. You’ll be out of here in no time at all.’ Later I find out he’s Professor Eisinger, at that time one of the top surgeons in the country. Anyway, I relax. I’m a lucky young man. I’ll be out of here in no time at all. And I feel fine, I’m not hurting anywhere. The doctors leave and I wonder why my parents aren’t here. Hasn’t anybody told them I’m here? This nurse comes in then and says that she has to change my dressings. What dressings? I ask myself. She pulls back the sheet. And my leg is gone. At first I don’t believe what I’m seeing, because I can still feel it. It feels like it’s there.”

Fifty years later and I could still hear the outrage, the shock, the pain in Gus’s voice as he looked down to where his leg had been. He seemed lost for a while before he picked up the story again.

“I started crying, carrying on, but the nurse grabbed me by the shoulders, and shook me hard. ‘You’re lucky to be alive,’ she said. ‘Now act like a man while I change your dressing.’”

"Maybe you were attacked by a great white," I said, thinking of the spate of shark attacks along the coast last year.

It was Gus's turn to fix me with a look. "It was The Debt, Dom."

"But what did they ask you to do? What was the repayment?"

Gus shook his head. "You know I can't tell you that," he said, a pained look on his face.

"But you have to tell me," I said. "I need to know what's going to happen to me."

Gus got up from his stool and stomped around on crutches for a while. Then he turned the radio on, really loud. Music was playing: Cold Chisel's "Khe Sahn." Gus moved in close to me, so close that I could smell his deodorant.

"The repayments are never the same," he said, his voice low. "Sometimes it's obvious what they, The Debt, stand to gain. Other times it's not so obvious. The repayment might seem more like a test of your mettle, to see what sort of man you are. But whatever you do, don't get too confident, don't get too cocky, not until you've finished the very last one."

Immediately I realized what had happened.

"That's the one you didn't do, isn't it? That's why they took your leg. But what was it, what did you have to do?"

"You know I can't tell you that," he said, as he took my empty bowl away.

I turned my attention back to *Running World*, but it was no good because Sebastian Coe's and Steve Ovett's achievements just didn't seem so awesome anymore.

Inside my head, thoughts were breeding thoughts, like microbes reproducing. What in the blazes had Gus's last installment been? And if Gus hadn't been able to repay it, then what chance did I have?

But there again, Dad had repaid his.

Had they been given the same installment? Was this why their relationship was so strained, why they always seemed to push each other's buttons?

Thoughts were breeding thoughts and it was getting too much, my head was ready to burst.

I had to get out of there.

I pushed my chair back. Got to my feet.

I threw a "See you later" in Gus's direction before I hurried outside.

Ω Ω Ω

As I walked next door to my house, I passed Roberto, the head gardener. As usual, he wasn't doing much gardening, just sitting on the riding mower, smoking a hand-rolled cigarette, talking on his mobile in Italian.

I guess he's about Dad's age, and he's worked – if that's the right word – for us ever since I can remember.

"Morning, Master Silvagni," he said when he saw me, a hint of sarcasm in his voice.

"Morning," I replied, before I continued on.

Toby, my thirteen-year-old brother, and Miranda, my sixteen-year-old sister, were in the kitchen, sitting at the table eating. Miranda was in a black bathrobe and black slippers, black flash drives – four of them – dangling around her neck. Toby was already in his school uniform, or his deconstructed version of the school uniform.

"Toby made pancakes," said Miranda loudly. "They're splendid."

"They're technically crepes," said Toby.

"I already ate ugali," I said.

"Yuck!" said Toby. "I don't know how you can eat that muck."

"Thirty million Kenyans eat that muck," I said.

"And Kenyan food is really up there, isn't it? Have you ever heard of a Kenyan restaurant? Ever heard of people ordering in Kenyan?"

Miranda just gave me one of her smiles; she's pretty used to her younger brothers going at it like this.

"See they caught the Zolt," I said.

She scoffed at that – and Miranda delivers pretty serious scoff.

"Not for long," she said.

She, like many teenage girls – with the honorable

exception of Imogen – is totally infatuated with the Zolt.

Mom came into the kitchen. If you've ever seen the episode "Pretty Angels All in a Row" in the TV series *Charlie's Angels,* then you've seen my mum.

In case you've forgotten, the Angels go undercover and become beauty contestants to find out who is scaring off the other contestants. In the scene where they're parading in Las Vegas, well, that's my mum behind Kelly and Sabrina, the one in the red bikini. Okay, you don't really see her face. And in the credits at the end, because of some union thing, she's listed under another name. But it is my mum.

Even now, because of her big hair, because of her Marilyn Monroe-style mole, because of her California accent, people will come up to her and say, "Weren't you in *Dallas*, or *Dynasty*, or *The Love Boat*?"

Her face will brighten, but then quickly fade again before she'll say, "No, that wasn't me."

"Oh," they'll say, disappointed.

"Sorry," Mom will say, equally disappointed.

A few weeks ago, when it happened again, Toby said to Mom, "You should just say you were in *Dallas*, no one's going to know the difference."

Mom's answer was really weird: "That's all we need, another lie."

She hasn't done any acting since she married Dad. Instead she runs this charity called the Angel

Foundation which takes some of the money Dad earns and gives it to the disadvantaged.

"Sweetheart, I'll pick you up after school to take you to the audition," Mom said to Toby.

"What audition?" I said.

"For *Ready! Set! Cook!* of course," said Mom, throwing Toby a winning smile.

In case you live under a rock or something, *Ready! Set! Cook!* is this TV program where the contestants compete against each other in cooking challenges. It's, like, the biggest rating program in the history of the universe and the winner is guaranteed to become filthy rich, appear in millions of ads and live happily ever after.

"Isn't he a bit young for *Ready! Set! Cook!*?" I said.

"It's *Junior Ready! Set! Cook!*" she said.

The only reply I could come up with was a pathetic "Oh."

"So when are you going to open the rest of your presents?" Toby asked, a smear of maple syrup glistening on his top lip.

"I'm not," I said. "I'm donating them to Mom's foundation."

"We're going to regift them," she said as she took out her BlackBerry.

"So your friends have spent hours and hours and hours searching for just the right present and you give it away without opening it?" said Toby.

"Seems like it."

Toby and I both knew that the presents I was donating, which were being regifted, weren't the ones from my friends. Mostly they were from my parents' friends, most of whom hardly knew me and had probably had them purchased by professional present buyers.

"I'm donating them," I said. "So you really need to install the Get Over It app on your phone."

"Even this one?" said Toby, bringing out from under the table a present wrapped in glossy gray paper. "I reckon it's a laptop."

"Who's it from?" I said.

Toby turned the present over in his hands before he said, "There's no card."

"Mom!" I said. She looked up from her BlackBerry. "Do you know who gave this to me?"

"Now, let me see. I do believe a courier dropped that off on your birthday."

"So there'd be paperwork somewhere?"

"Over there, sweetheart," she said, pointing to a stack of manila folders on a side table. "There's a folder with your name on it."

Indeed there was – *Dom's 15th Birthday* was DYMO-labeled on the cover – and inside I found the docket from the courier. My name was in the recipient's box. And in the sender's box were two words: *The Debt*.

I closed my eyes, but when I opened them again those two words were still there.

I guess my mind had been resisting the idea of The Debt all along. It was too outlandish, too unbelievable. Despite the brand inside my thigh, despite Elliott dead and broken on the pavement, despite the evidence that said The Debt was real and imminent and dangerous, I kept thinking that it would go away and life would return to normal. But here was more evidence; and furthermore, there was nothing ambiguous about it. They, The Debt, the 'Ndrangheta, had sent me a birthday present!

"Okay," I said to Toby. "Let's see what it is."

It'd been shrink-wrapped and I needed a sharp knife to pry off the covering.

"I told you it was a laptop!" said Toby.

Maybe, but its case was like no other I'd seen. It was matte black, made from some sort of burnished metal.

"What type is it?" asked Miranda from the other side of the table, removing the iPhone buds from her ears.

"I'm not sure," I said.

"PC or Mac?" said Miranda.

Again, I wasn't sure. I handed the laptop to Miranda.

She turned it around in her hands, the look of puzzlement on her face growing.

"It's got USB ports," she said, "but no Ethernet. No power inlet, either. That's strange, it must be totally wireless. But how do you open it?"

I could see what she meant: there were no buttons, no latches, nothing that interrupted its smooth hi-tech surface.

"It's like a clam," said Miranda.

"A ClamTop," said Toby, laughing, pleased with his own joke.

"Maybe it's voice-activated," said Miranda.

She put the ClamTop on the table, and said, "Open."

The ClamTop remained resolutely shut.

"What about 'Open Sesame'?" said Miranda.

Nothing happened.

"Or 'Open Extra-Virgin Sesame Oil'?" said Toby, opting for even more humor.

"Or touch activated," said Miranda, running her hands over its surface.

Again, it didn't work.

"Time for school, you lot," said Mom, putting away her BlackBerry.

I took the ClamTop up to my room and put it on my desk. As I got ready for school I kept sneaking glances at it.

If I'd doubted The Debt before I couldn't doubt it now, because here was the proof that it existed.

There was a cursory knock on my door before

Miranda barged in, flash drives jangling.

"I need to have another squiz at that thing," she said, picking up the ClamTop.

"Give it here," I said.

Miranda kept hold of the ClamTop, a defiant look on her face.

"It's my present, give it to me," I demanded.

More defiance from Miranda, but then Mom's voice came from downstairs. "We're leaving in five, people!"

Miranda handed me the ClamTop and hurried back out of my room.

A FORMALITY

As the ten of us on the Coast Boys Grammar track team got changed in one corner of the locker room, everybody was joking and mucking about. Well, everybody except Rashid, who was his usual hyper-serious self. I looked over at Seb and thought it was a shame he wasn't eligible, because then we really would have a race on our hands. As it was, the result was pretty much a foregone conclusion. All season there'd been four of us – Rashid, Gabby, Charles and me – who had clearly been the best performers and deserved a shot at the state titles. Even if one of us fell over, or sprained an ankle, none of the other members of the team would run past him, finish before him. Okay, maybe Bevan Milne would. That's because Bevan Milne was a bit of a turd.

"Coming in, boys!" came Coach Sheeds's voice from outside the locker room.

Which meant that you had about a millisecond to get unnaked if you were naked, unless you were Charles and you just didn't care. "She's a lesbian," he'd say. "It's not a big thing to her."

Although Charles Bonthron looks like a surfer – he's tanned, he's blond, he's scruffy – and although he talks like a surfer – "I was, like, totally stoked" – he is actually from Grammar royalty. His family has been coming to this school since it was first formed, when the Gold Coast was all Coast and no Gold. Our running track – the Bill Bonthron Running Track – was named after his great-grandfather, and a great-uncle of his won bronze in the mile at the Auckland Commonwealth Games. If it weren't for the patronage of his family, we probably wouldn't even have a track team and we definitely wouldn't have any athletics scholarships.

Coach Sheeds appeared with Tristan Jazy by her side. A smirk on his face, a sports bag in his hand, he towered over her.

What was he doing here?

"You all know Tristan?" said Coach Sheeds.

It was a rhetorical question, because everybody in the school knows Tristan Jazy, or is aware of his accomplishments. He was the youngest boy ever to play in the senior rugby team. He'd scored a century off twenty-eight balls in the interschool cricket competition. He was a state-ranked swimmer.

"Tristan's going to run with us today," said Coach Sheeds.

Once a world-ranked 5000 meter runner, Coach Sheeds has the poker face of a professional athlete, and I couldn't tell whether she was pleased or as perturbed as I was by this revelation.

"But he's not even on the track team," I blurted.

Only the other day Tristan had been telling me how useless track running was, how it was for wusses who were scared of getting hurt playing a real sport.

"Tristan is a member of our school body," said Coach Sheeds, "so there's nothing to stop him from joining us today."

"You worried you going to get your butt kicked, Domino?" said Tristan, moving next to me so that he could give me a playful punch on the arm.

Playful for him, painful for me.

With that, Coach Sheeds left us to get changed. There was no joking now, no mucking about, and the only person talking was Tristan.

"Look at those guns, will you?" he said, flexing his admittedly impressive biceps.

Followed by, "And how's that for a six pack?" as he peeled off his shirt.

And then, grabbing his crotch, "No wonder the chicks are lining up for a bit of Tristan action."

What chicks? What action?

Seb nudged me with his elbow, and mouthed, "Moron."

"Prize," I added.

"How about you close your mouth now?" Rashid said to Tristan in his less-than-perfect English. "We need to think before big race."

Rashid's parents are Afghani refugees and he's at the school on a scholarship. Which was something the school never seems to get tired of mentioning in its newsletter. But it also meant that he was under pressure to perform.

"What was that?" said Tristan with exaggerated enunciation.

Cupping his ear, he moved closer to where Rashid was sitting. "Sorry, but I only speak English."

Rashid stood up. Though he's a big kid, with a keg of a chest, Tristan's way bigger than him, way bigger than all of us.

It was like somebody had decided to build a skyscraper in a country town.

"You know the score, Abdul. I grew here and you flew here. Actually, I'm wrong, you're one of those boat people, aren't you?"

Rashid tensed, moving closer to Tristan.

"Hey, you're probably one of those kids they threw overboard," said Tristan.

"That's enough," said Seb, stepping between the two much bigger boys just when Rashid decided to punch, or attempt to punch, Tristan's skyscraper lights out.

Somehow Rashid's fist caught Seb on the nose. His head snapped back and blood immediately began pouring from one nostril.

"Look what you've done now, Abdul," taunted Tristan.

Both Rashid and I went to Seb's aid.

"I'm sorry," said a mortified Rashid.

"Here, use this," I said, handing Seb my towel.

"Thanks," he said, holding it to his face.

"We better see the doctor," said Rashid. "Nose might be destroyed."

"I'm running," said Seb.

"But –" I tried.

"I'm running."

It was no use arguing; nothing was going to stop Seb from running, from showing Coach Sheeds what he had. I ducked into the cubicle, grabbed the roll of toilet paper, came out and handed it to Seb. He understood, disappearing back into the cubicle. He reappeared with a swollen nose and a nostril bulging with paper, but at least the flow had stopped.

"Just don't let Coach see you," I said, "or she won't let you run."

"Come on, boys!" came Coach Sheeds's voice from outside. "Time to boogie."

She got us all together at the long jump pit for one of her little pep talks, opening with what I liked to think of as her Hakuna Matata, though there was nothing really Hakuna Matataesque about it.

"Every morning in Africa a gazelle wakes up knowing it must run faster than the fastest lion, or it will be killed. Every morning in Africa a lion wakes up knowing it must run faster than the slowest gazelle, or it will starve."

As she Hakuna Matata-ed away, I looked at my fellow competitors. They, like me, had heard this a thousand times before, but they were still intent on every word.

Not me, however.

I couldn't stop thinking about the ClamTop, about how to open it. And what if I couldn't open it? What then? Dad had repaid all six installments. Gus had repaid five. Would I even repay one?

I focused on Coach Sheeds, determined that I wasn't going to let The Debt distract me from my dream to be a champion runner.

She ended with one of her favorite sayings: "Pain is inevitable, suffering is optional, boys."

Afterwards, she took me aside.

"Champ, I'm thinking four-o-six will do the job today," she said.

As in four minutes and six seconds.

"Keep the splits to around sixty-two and show us your usual kick."

"And Tristan?"

"Tristan?"

"Yeah, what time are you thinking for Tristan?"

"Look, I didn't ask him to run, okay?" said Coach Sheeds.

I wasn't too sure if she was telling the truth or not. Getting a star like Tristan involved in the track team would be a big feather in her cap, and lately Coach Sheeds's cap was sporting about as much plumage as a battery hen.

Coach Sheeds continued. "Besides, if that rumor about the Kenyans is right, then you need all the competition you can get."

The rumor was that Brisbane Boys School, our archenemy, had imported some Kenyans to juice up their track team.

"On your marks!" said the starter, and as we took our positions at the starting line I noticed that there were quite a few people in the stands.

For one second I allowed myself a fantasy: middle distance running had suddenly become as popular as rugby, as sexy as surfing, but then I noticed that all the kids looked around the same size, the same age.

Obviously a teacher had brought his class down, and I had a pretty good idea which teacher it was:

Mr. Ryan. As far as I knew he was the only one who had any interest in running.

"Ready!" said the starter.

The gun went off.

Rashid was straightaway in the lead.

Charles tucked in behind him.

And then Tristan.

I had to admit he looked pretty good. He was a bit stiff, but a lot of footballers are like that when they run. All those muscles they grew in the gym might come in handy for busting through tackles, for scrummaging or whatever they called it, but they just get in the way with middle distance running. Still, Tristan had an uncomplicated running style, and he had a hungry stride that gobbled up the tarmac. Seb, Gabby and I sat behind him. And behind us Bevan Milne, that bit of a turd, headed the pack.

We ran the first lap in sixty-two seconds and the race was going to plan. The four of us on the team had put at least twenty meters on the pack. So had Seb. And so had Tristan.

Suddenly a thought occurred to me: though he wasn't on the team, Tristan must still be eligible to represent the school at the state titles. And wouldn't the school love that: Tristan Jazy, champion rugby player, champion cricketer, champion swimmer, now champion runner. How good would that look on the front page of the school newsletter?

We had to drop him, or one of us – Rashid, Charles, Gabby or even me – would miss out. We'd trained all season together, done all that gym work together, run in the rain together, run through mud together – none of us deserved to miss out.

I ran up beside Rashid.

"Put some pace on, we need to drop Tristan."

Rashid smiled at me: he likes dropping people no matter who they are, but I reckoned dropping Tristan would be especially satisfying. Immediately he increased the pace. We did the next lap in a brisk sixty seconds, and by then the pack had fallen way back.

Not Tristan, though.

He wasn't running pretty, his head was tilting to one side, but he was breathing easy, not "sucking in the big ones," as Gus would say. I was thinking about what we should do when Tristan tilted his head a little more to one side and took off. All the great middle distance runners do this, run in spurts. But who did Tristan think he was? Filbert Bayi?

I looked over at Gabby.

"Let him go," he said. "He'll run out of steam."

"Anyway, he's not eligible," added Charles.

But if he didn't run out of steam, if he was eligible, if he won the race, or even finished in the first four, then one of us would miss out.

I waited for another half lap.

Tristan hadn't run out of steam; in fact he now had at least a two-hundred-meter lead.

I had no choice, I took off after him.

As I did I could feel footsteps behind me.

A quick glance over my shoulder revealed that it was Seb.

"Let's get the prize moron," he said.

The plug of tissue paper had worked itself loose from his nostril and blood was flowing again, rivulets of it running down his face, down his neck.

We ran like Kenyans, taking it in turns to lead until, with one lap to go, we caught Tristan.

Now it was me who was sucking in the big ones.

"What the blazes are you doing?" I asked as I ran alongside Tristan.

"Showing you wusses how it's done," he said, and there was this strange, wired look in his eyes.

Still a hundred meters to go, too far to start sprinting for the finish. I had no choice, though, because I had to blow Tristan up so that the others could catch him. I went up a gear, took off.

Eighty meters later and it was me who blew up, me who hit the wall.

Tristan cruised past me.

Then Rashid, Charles, Gabby.

Seb came up alongside.

"You okay?" he asked.

"I'm gone," I gasped.

"We're almost there," he said.

I looked over at Seb, saw that his singlet was now crimson with blood.

"Come on!" he said.

I glanced behind – the pack was drawing closer and that turd Bevan Milne was at the front.

I found some fuel, found a gear, and forced my legs to move.

Seb and I crossed the finish line together.

And I collapsed on the ground, chest heaving.

"What the blazes happened out there?" Coach Sheeds asked me when I eventually managed to drag myself back to my feet.

"It's only the stupid state titles," I said.

"What are you talking about?"

"I finished fifth, I didn't qualify."

"Of course you did."

"So Tristan wasn't eligible then?"

"Of course not. Like I told you, he just wanted to have a run."

Thanks for telling me, Coach Sheeds.

She continued. "But what a run, eh? Wouldn't I love to get my hands on a talent like that?"

As Seb and I walked to the bus stop, he said, "Do you know that Mr. Ryan dude?"

"Sure, he's one of my teachers. Why?"

"He was talking to me after the race. Said I should try out for the cross-country team. That I'd have more chance of a scholarship with them."

"Bull you would," I said.

Seb didn't say anything to that and we walked in silence for a while, but then I remembered something.

"Hey, it's your birthday today, isn't it?"

He smiled. "We're the same age now."

As he said this a black car veered out of the traffic and pulled up alongside us. Cars – or vans – may not be my thing but I knew this one: it was a Subaru WRX, and it was sporting Learner plates. The back door swung open.

The Debt, I thought. The last thing I wanted was for Seb to get mixed up in all that.

"You keep going," I said. "I'll handle this."

"It's okay," he said.

I watched him get into the backseat of the car and close the door before the WRX took off with a burble of its exhaust.

HYPOTENUSE THE CAT

"I reckon Pythagoras was this nasty old Greek dude who hated kids," I said to Imogen.

We were in my room, sprawled out on the carpet doing homework, like we did most school nights. My house is pretty much the only place Imogen is allowed to visit. Well, we were supposed to be doing our homework. Imogen had the newspaper open in front of her, a marker in her hand. She was going through the photos, one at a time, looking closely at each person before she put a neat cross over his or her face.

Imogen looked up from the newspaper and said, "Please don't say 'dude,'" before she returned to the paper, crossing out another face, this one belonging to the winner of the Best Director category in this year's Academy Awards.

I continued. "So he comes up with this theorem in order to torture us. Thousands of years since he died and he's still torturing us."

"I like 'hypotenuse,' said Imogen. "If Mum lets me get a cat this year I'm going to call it Hypotenuse."

"You'd end up calling it Hypie," I said. "Or Hypo."

Imogen considered that for a while before she said, "You should be good at triangles."

"Why's that?"

"Because when you run, that's what you look like. All triangles. Like a collision of triangles."

A collision of triangles? I wasn't sure whether I should be flattered or not.

Imogen pointed at one of the questions in my remedial math book.

"What about this one?" she said. "A is eight, b is six, how long is c?"

"I don't know, you're the one with the cat called Hypotenuse. You work it out, Im."

"Me working it out isn't going to get you up to speed in math."

"I don't want to get up to speed in math, you know that. I just want to run really freaking fast for four laps, win Olympic gold medals and break Hicham El Guerrouj's world records for the mile and the fifteen hundred."

As I said this the words seemed hollow. I'd just had my butt kicked by Tristan, and he wasn't even a serious runner. Imogen closed the newspaper and put the cap on the pen.

"Okay, I'll do the problem, but you have to sign my petition."

"I already did," I said, thinking of the petition she had to let kids play on the grass in the Halcyon Grove Lifestyle Precinct.

"No, this is a new one. I want Halcyon Grove to turn off their lights for Earth Hour. The last one was shameful."

I wasn't so sure about shameful. A bit embarrassing maybe.

"Okay, I'll sign it, but it won't do any good," I said.

The body corporate hadn't taken any notice of Imogen's many petitions. In fact, they'd put even more "Do Not Step on the Grass" signs in the lifestyle precinct after the last one. Imogen frowned and looked down at the problem in the math book.

"So c squared equals eight squared plus six squared, which equals sixty-four plus thirty-six, which equals a hundred. So c equals the square root of a hundred, which is ten. C equals ten."

"Total voodoo," I said, writing the answer in my book. "How was school today?"

"It was okay," said Imogen. "I came top of my class in pretty much everything."

"Wow!" I said. "What about the school swimming carnival?"

"Yeah, won everything again."

"Athletics?"

"Didn't lose a race."

"School formal?"

"It's going to go off."

In case you don't get it: Imogen is homeschooled by a variety of teachers and tutors who come to her home.

"Do you reckon your mum will let you go to a real school next year?" I said.

My mum had been working on it, talking to Imogen's mother, telling her how important it was that Imogen mixed with other kids her age. Imogen sighed, a sigh that seemed to come from somewhere with no shortage of despair and despondency.

"We could even give you a lift," I said.

Another of those sighs. Mrs. Havilland never goes outside. Outside her house. Outside Halcyon Grove. Outside anywhere. Because the last time she did, her husband, Imogen's father, my dad's best friend, disappeared.

The Havillands had gone to Taverniti's, this expensive restaurant on Main Beach, to celebrate Mr. Havilland's reelection as the local state MP. Just before dessert, Mr. Havilland went outside to take a phone call, and he didn't come back. They searched for him, of course, in Taverniti's, all along the Coast, all over the country, all over the world, but there was no trace. It was like he just vaporized, dematerialized.

Imogen went through the newspaper every day, looking for her dad's face, crossing out those that weren't his.

"The last question," she said, getting up from the floor. "The answer's six. C equals six."

I wrote that down as Imogen's phone beeped. She checked the message and smiled.

"Who's that from?" I asked.

"None of your business," she said.

"What do you mean, it's none of my business?" I said, and I wasn't joking.

Imogen and I have known each other forever; our mothers were pregnant with us at the same time. We went to the same preschool. Went to the same kindergarten. Even went to the same primary school until Mrs. Havilland took Imogen out. Her business was my business. And vice versa, of course.

Imogen ignored my question and was busy typing a reply to the message, thumbs flying.

"Come on," I said. "Who is it?"

"If you must know, it's Tristan."

"What does that moron want?"

Looking offended, Imogen said, "Tristan's okay."

It was only two words, and two pretty innocent words at that, but their combined effect was devastating.

Tristan wasn't okay and hadn't been since his family had moved in next door to the Havillands. I remembered sitting with Imogen that day, watching Tristan strut around. She'd turned to me and said, "Not okay" and that was it – it instantly became another part of our shared language, like rap is crap, sharks are cool, and under no circumstances should dads ever be allowed to wear Speedos.

Tristan wasn't okay and could never be okay. He should be put in a museum somewhere, behind glass, with a sign that said *Not okay*. But now, all of a sudden, that had changed and it felt like a betrayal.

As Imogen sent the message I remembered Tristan's crotch-grabbing words: "No wonder the chicks are lining up for a bit of Tristan action."

Imogen pointed at the ClamTop. "What's that?"

"Computer," I said, opting for an I'm-unhappy-with-you-so-am-only-going-to-give-the-briefest-of-answers approach.

"Where'd it come from?"

"Birthday present."

"How do you open it?"

"Dunno."

At various times Miranda had popped into my room with her latest hot theory as to how to crack the ClamTop. None of which had been successful.

"Not even Miranda can work it out," I said, getting sick of the-briefest-of-answers approach.

Straight after school my sister had brought over a couple of her fellow geeks, one of whom had used a stethoscope to examine the ClamTop in the same way a doctor examines a patient. I almost expected him to say, "Cough, please." But he didn't manage to open it, either.

"Oh, that's how," said Imogen.

I looked around to see that the clam had unclammed – the laptop had opened!

"What did you do?" I asked, jumping to my feet.

"I was nice to it," said Imogen.

The screen was like no other screen I'd ever seen. Darker, blacker, deeper.

"How do you boot it up?" asked Imogen.

"Be even nicer to it?" I suggested.

I touched the screen gently with my forefinger, causing a fluorescent blue light to glow. As I moved my finger across the screen, the blue light became a blue line.

"That's cool," said Imogen.

I agreed – it was cool, but that's all it was, because when I removed my finger the blue line disappeared.

How do you actually communicate with this thing?

Suddenly, across the screen, the words *Dom, catch the Zolt!* appeared in the same deep blue.

I looked over at Imogen; she didn't seem to have noticed.

"Look," I said, pointing at the screen.

"Yeah, blank screen. Big deal."

"Can't you see the writing?"

"What writing?"

"Stand next to me," I said, thinking that perhaps it was the angle she was looking from. She did as I asked.

"Dom, there's nothing there."

She really couldn't see it.

Dom, catch the Zolt!

But the Zolt had already been caught. How was I supposed to communicate that? There was no keyboard, in its place was what looked like another screen. I ran my finger across it. Nothing happened. With no input device, how was I supposed to communicate with it? I remembered what Miranda had said when we first unwrapped it: maybe it was voice activated.

I looked straight at the screen and said, enunciating slowly, "How can I catch the Zolt if he's already been caught?"

"Are you talking to the computer?" Imogen asked.

But it worked. Sort of.

You must catch the Zolt by the end of the month! was now written across the screen.

Again, I looked at the screen and said, "But he's already been caught."

"Dom, you're starting to seriously freak me out," said Imogen.

Catch the Zolt by the end of the month! appeared on the screen.

"Okay, and what do I do with him when I've caught him?" I asked.

Catch the Zolt by the end of the month!

For a computer, it was being annoyingly vague.

"Why should I?"

Two flashing words only.

THE DEBT.

The ClamTop snapped shut.

FAMILY PHOTOS

The next day, when the heinous Baha Men went off, I did nothing. Just lay in bed, becoming part of the morning stillness. My body felt stiff and sore, drained of all energy after yesterday's race, and the scabby brand on the inside of my thigh ached. Yesterday, losing had seemed the most disastrous of all disasters, but today it seemed unimportant, almost trivial.

I thought of Imogen. "Tristan's okay," she'd said, and I still couldn't quite believe that those words had come out of her mouth.

Rap is crap. Sharks are cool. Under no circumstances should dads ever be allowed to wear Speedos. And Tristan was so not okay!

And I thought about The Debt, about my first installment, my first assignment. I recalled what Gus had told me, that the repayment might seem more like a test of my mettle, to see what sort of man I was. But how could I catch somebody who had already been caught?

As more and more morning light found its way into my room, the inside of my head became darker and darker. I needed to talk to somebody, so I got dressed and walked over to Gus's place. I let myself in.

"Gus! You there, Gus?"

There was no answer.

That's strange. Where can he be?

Usually at this time I was running, so maybe he always went out, but he'd never mentioned it. I checked the garage: his truck was gone. I checked his office: his leg was gone.

The new edition of *Running World* was on his desk, so I sat down to read it.

As I did, I noticed that there was a pile of printouts from the Internet. They all seemed to be concerned with biochips, tiny silicon chips that were implanted in the human body.

Gus really is turning into a nerd.

But even so, why would he be interested in something like this? Even before I'd finished asking myself the question, I knew the answer: as a training tool, of course. Imagine being able to track a runner's every move, to instantly calculate the distance they'd covered?

As I thumbed through the printouts my mind wandered, taking me back into the past, to when Gus first arrived at Halcyon Grove.

I was eight when Dad said that we were going to have an important family meeting. Now we weren't one of those families, like the Silversteins, that were always having family meetings. Somebody didn't replace the toilet paper? Call a family meeting. Light left on? Family meeting. No, a family meeting was a big deal for us. So even now, seven years later, I could remember it clearly.

It was about eight at night, but, because it was summer, it was still light. The five of us were sitting around the kitchen table. Close to me was a fruit bowl, with two mangoes in it. I'm not sure why, but I always remember those two mangoes.

Dad looked uncharacteristically nervous.

"Kids," he said, "your mother and I have something to tell you that is going to come as a bit of a shock."

Mom, arms folded, lips compressed, was looking out the window.

"I know I've told you on a number of occasions that your grandfather and grandmother, my parents, passed away before any of you were born."

Dad took time to establish eye contact with each of us kids before he said, "Well, I lied to you. Your grandfather is alive."

I remember, right then, focusing on those two mangoes.

My grandfather was alive?

"Can you get me some water, sweetheart?" Dad asked Mom.

Mom hesitated before she poured the water, some of it sloshing over the side of the glass. Dad took a sip and continued.

"I haven't told you children that much about my childhood, but you've probably realized that it wasn't … well, it wasn't …"

Dad took another sip of water and I could see the tears forming in his eyes. "Put it this way, it wasn't what you kids have." He waved his hand, indicating the enormous house we lived in, the expensive cars in the driveway, the glittering pool.

"But if our grandfather's alive, where is he?" asked Miranda.

"Yeah, where is he?" added Toby.

I said nothing. I couldn't. This grandfather-back-from-the-dead revelation was almost too much for me to process.

Dad and Mom looked at each other, before Dad said, "Well, he's been in South America. But very soon he's going to be next door."

"Your father bought the Dowd house," said Mom, and I could tell from the tone of her voice that she wasn't happy about this.

But I also remember thinking that it was a relief to hear her voice, as I was starting to worry that Dad had lost his mind or something, because he wasn't making much sense.

"And this grandfather of yours will be moving into it," said Mom.

Which is exactly what happened.

Dad had told us about Gus's missing leg, but there's a big difference between being told about something and actually experiencing it. And then there was Gus himself: if he'd been happy about being brought back from the dead, he certainly didn't show it. He'd seemed shy, almost embarrassed.

Then I saw it, sitting on the desk. Gus must've forgotten to put it back. The key to the desk drawer. I placed it into the keyhole, turned it. A click. I slid the drawer open. The red leather binder was there. I took it out. Opened it.

The Debt.

I removed *Pagherò Cambiario* from its plastic sleeve. Ran my fingers across its surface. Held it up to the light. The paper was thin; the light streamed through it. I could've torn it into a thousand pieces. Put a match to it and watched it go *whoosh!*

But I didn't. Instead, I used my iPhone to take a photo of the document. I was about to put the binder back in the bottom drawer when I noticed the edge of another binder. I pulled the drawer further out.

This binder was also leather, but it didn't look as old as the other one. It was also bulging with material, zipped shut. Guiltily, I took it out.

If my grandfather had wanted me to see this, he would've shown me, I thought.

I placed it on the desk, unzipped it. Clippings, papers, photos spilled out. I picked up the first photo. A boy in old-fashioned running gear. Except for the clothes, it could have been me: the same long legs, the same angular face, the same mop of thick black hair. I remembered what Imogen said about me looking like a "collision of triangles."

I turned it over. Written on the back was *Giuseppe Silvagni, 15*.

It must've been taken just before he lost his leg.

Even as I thought this I realized that I still didn't believe that The Debt, the 'Ndrangheta, whatever you wanted to call them, had taken their pound of flesh, had taken Gus's leg. It just wasn't possible. Not in the twentieth century. Not in Australia.

The next photo was also in black and white, of a family.

"We lost most of the family photos in a fire," Gus had told me when I was researching that school project. "It was a terrible thing."

In the background of the photo was a house, surrounded by sugarcane, though "house" is probably too grand a word for something that was

more like a shack, that looked like it was made from scraps of corrugated iron and burlap sacking.

I knew Gus's family had been poor sugarcane farmers, but I hadn't realized that they'd been this poor. I focused my attention on the people standing self-consciously in front of the house. Immediately I recognized Gus. He was shoeless, shirtless, and looked as though he was about ten or eleven years old. Next to him were two other boys, similarly dressed.

They looked younger than Gus, perhaps by a couple of years, and they looked like twins. Not identical, but the same height, the same sharp features. They were Gus's brothers. They had to be: the resemblance was unmistakable. They all looked alike. They all looked like me.

But how many times had Gus told me, when I was complaining about Miranda or Toby, that I was lucky to have a brother and a sister because he'd been brought up as an only child?

Maybe these kids were cousins, or some other relatives, I thought.

I studied the photo again. No, they were his brothers; I had no doubt about that. Behind the three children were two adults. Gus's mother, my great-grandmother, looked old and worn. The man, Gus's father, glared fiercely at the camera, as if he somehow resented the photographer. He had his arms folded tightly in front of his chest, so that his hands weren't visible.

Just then came the sound of a car pulling into the garage. I stuffed the papers and photos back into the binder and zipped it up. Shoved it into the desk, locked the drawer and put the key back where I found it. Just as I picked up the copy of *Running World*, Gus entered.

"Blazing bells and buckets of blood!" he said, startled. "You scared the crap out of me! What are you doing here?"

"I didn't run this morning," I said, a pretty blatant statement of the obvious.

I saw Gus's eyes take in the key on his desk.

I may not have run that morning, but my heart was racing.

"They've given me the first installment," I blurted.

Immediately I could see the concern on Gus's face.

"They want me –" I started, but Gus stopped me from going any further by saying, "I don't want to know."

"It's impossible!" I said.

Gus took a while to answer.

"It's not impossible, it's –"

"It *is* impossible!"

"It may seem impossible, but it's not. You've got to think of it in business terms. No creditor wants to

destroy its debtors, because then there's no chance they can make their repayments."

I thought about that. It made sense except for one thing.

"They destroyed you," I said.

As soon as I said this, I wished I hadn't, because Gus seemed to shrivel before my eyes.

I was about to apologize, to tell him that wasn't really what I meant, when my phone started ringing, playing "You're the One That I Want."

I knew it was Imogen calling because the week before Miranda and Toby, amusing siblings that they were, had taken my phone and given Imogen her own ringtone.

And I hadn't bothered to change it because, let's face it, she *was* the one that I wanted. Perhaps just not with the *uh uh uhs*. Okay, maybe even with the *uh uh uhs*.

"Hi, Dom," said The One That I Want. "What you doing after school?"

"Not much," I said. "You want to hang out?"

"Well, there is this thing ..."

"What thing?"

"Can't really say," she whispered conspiratorially, as if our phones were being bugged by one of those spy agencies like ASIO, or the CIA, or Google. "Probably better if you come over and I can explain."

"I'll be there at four," I said, before I hung up.

Gus was still standing there.

We looked at each other. I shrugged.

"I didn't mean what I said to you."

He shrugged. "This Debt business is a bugger."

We both agreed: a real bugger, before we went our separate ways.

WAILING

When I pressed the buzzer it was Imogen's mother's voice that crackled over the intercom. "Who is it?"

"Dom," I replied.

"Oh," she said, and it almost seemed as if she was disappointed, as if she had been expecting somebody a bit more threatening, like Freddy Krueger or the *Texas Chainsaw Massacre* dude.

"Come in," she said.

When I opened the door she was standing well back, wearing a dressing gown and fluffy slippers.

Mrs. Havilland, like Mom, had been an actress. But while strangers still come up to Mom to ask if she was on TV, nobody comes up to Mrs. Havilland. For a start, she doesn't go outside. And she doesn't look much like a TV star anymore.

"Hello, Mrs. Havilland," I said.

"Dom," she said. "Haven't you shot up?"

Enough with the shooting up already.

She continued, "How's your mum?"

"She's good."

"She hasn't dropped in for a while. She must be very busy."

"Very busy," I said, but then I thought of something.

"When did you first meet my mum?" I asked.

"A long time ago," said Mrs. Havilland, doing that thing adults do that I hate, making out that they're incredibly, immeasurably old, that they were actually around when Gondwanaland split, when dinosaurs became extinct, when TVs didn't have remotes.

"You met on a show in Sydney or something, didn't you?" I asked, and as I did something occurred to me: I didn't actually know that much about my mum, about her past. What I did know were the same old stories: *Charlie's Angels*, walking into Taverniti's and seeing scruffy Dad, falling in love with him and getting married.

Mrs. Havilland thought about my question for a while, but all she could come up with was, "It was such a long time ago."

Pre-remotes, pre-dinosaur-extinction, pre-Gondwanaland-split.

"But do you have, like, newspaper clippings or anything?" I asked.

Mrs. Havilland was about to answer, but she was interrupted by Imogen's voice from upstairs. "Is that you, Dom?"

"Yes, it's me," I called.

"Clippings?" said Mrs. Havilland.

"Yes, from when you and Mom were in that show."

"I'll see what I can find," she said.

Imogen appeared at the top of the stairs, looking beautiful, looking radiant, looking Imogenic.

I followed her into her room, but it wasn't the Imogen I'd known forever, the Imogen I'd gone to kindergarten with, the Imogen the four-year-old me was certain he would marry one day.

That Imogen was calm, this Imogen was all over the place. That Imogen didn't talk much, this Imogen wouldn't shut up. There were multiple hugs, and thank-you-so-much-for-coming repeated about a thousand times, before she said, "We have to go to Town Hall Square."

Town Hall Square is the place people go when they want to get together to celebrate or to protest.

"How come?"

"It's a party."

"For what?"

Imogen didn't answer, just gave me this sort of guilty look.

"But what's the party for?" I said.

"Promise not to get mad?" she said.

"Mad at what?"

"Just promise."

"Okay, I, Dominic Silvagni, hereby swear that I will hereby not get mad."

"Otto escaped," she said, and the affectionate way she said "Otto" made it sound as though she'd known him forever, as if it was he who was her soul mate, not me.

"The Zolt escaped?" I said.

Imogen handed me her iPhone.

Twitter was like a canary on amphetamines.

zolt has excaped.

zolt has dissapeared.

hound davillieer has bean found naked in boat smeared in nutella.

Over and over again, the same message retweeted.

zolt excaped

zolt dissapeared

hound davillieer naked in boat smeared in nutella

"He really has escaped?" I said.

Imogen smiled, and said, "You doubted him?" but I wasn't really listening to her anymore.

Catch the Zolt!

I had my first installment.

Okay, that was big, about as BIG as it gets, and for a few seconds, maybe even longer, I was enveloped in its BIGNESS.

But then something else.

"You and the Zolt?" I said looking hard at Imogen.

Whenever I'd said how crazy all this Zolt-love was, she'd always agreed with me.

Imogen looked even more guilty. "I was going to tell you," she said, "but I thought you'd think I was silly."

You didn't have to be a psychiatrist, psychologist, a psych-anything to understand why Imogen would adore the Zolt. He was free and she wasn't.

"In your case, I'm willing to make an exception," I said, smiling at my once-future wife. "Who's coming to this thing, anyway?"

"Everybody."

"Everybody?"

"Well, everybody on Facebook," she said, and then she had this look on her face, as if she was deciding something.

Eventually she said, "Promise not to get mad," again.

"I already promised not get mad, remember," I said.

"But that was for something else. Promise again."

"Okay, I hereby promise again."

"Tristan's coming," she said.

"Tristan!" I said with as much contempt as I could muster.

"You hereby promised," warned Imogen.

"Okay," I said. "Let's go meet the now-apparently-okay Tristan. And then, after, we can listen to some rap, preferably of the hardcore gangsta variety. And then congratulate all those dads wearing Speedos."

Imogen glared at me, but there was still a half smile on her face.

"And it's okay with your mum?" I said.

Imogen gave me an are-you-kidding? look before she said, "Can you help me sneak out?"

All the times I'd wanted Imogen to sneak out – to the opening of the new Styxx shop downtown, to see me race – and she wouldn't because she didn't want to upset her mum. Now she wanted me to help her sneak out to see, of all people, of all creeps, Tristan.

Still, it only took me about a nanosecond to say, "Okay, I'll help you."

And let's face it, it was also a pretty perfect opportunity for me to learn about the Zolt. But it wasn't as if I was going to get off my shiny white high horse to inform Imogen of that, though.

No, I was doing her the mother of all favors.

Because Mrs. Havilland spent the day downstairs in bed, mostly watching television or doing crosswords, you wouldn't have thought that sneaking out would be particularly difficult. But she's like a spider who had spun an invisible web, whose filaments reached into every nook and cranny of the house. She can hear, feel, every little vibration. Sneaking out wasn't going to be easy.

I checked out the window.

It was a long way down.

If only this was a movie, I thought. There would be convenient gutters to clamber down, convenient trees to climb into.

There were a few handholds, a few footholds, and I was confident I could make it down, but I wasn't so sure about Imogen. Strangers came up to her and offered to make her the world's next supermodel, not the world's next super-athlete.

"We could knot the sheets together," said Imogen. "Climb out through the window."

We could, but it would mean that the knotted sheets would be left dangling.

In Halcyon Grove it would take no time at all before somebody reported it and security came knocking at the door. Scaring the crap – or what was left of it – out of poor Mrs. Havilland.

In the end I went downstairs and knocked on the half-opened door to Mrs. Havilland's bedroom.

"Come in," she said.

Mrs. Havilland was on the bed, propped up by pillows, smoking. The room smelled of perfume and cigarettes. The television was on.

"And haven't you got the peachiest complexion?" said one of the characters in a voice I sort of recognized.

I turned my attention to the screen. Now I realized

why the voice was familiar: it belonged to a much-younger Mrs. Havilland. Who was wearing a halter top and a miniskirt.

"Is that you?" I said.

"Yes, that was me." Mrs. Havilland exhaled a long thin stream of smoke.

"Wow, Mrs. Havilland, you were hot," I said.

"I was, wasn't I?" She seemed to drift off for a moment, then she hit the off button on the remote control and the video ceased whirring.

Okay, Dominic, out with it.

I took a deep breath and blurted, "Imogen and I would like to go to the city."

Mrs. Havilland looked shocked. "The city? Do you realize how much crime there is in the city?"

I half nodded, half shrugged.

"I'd look after her," I said, drawing myself up to my full height, the full height the runner in me wasn't particularly pleased with.

Mrs. Havilland took another deep drag of her cigarette. "And how do you intend to get there?"

"Buses," I replied, but I realized that probably wasn't the right answer, so I added, "a taxi if we have to."

She considered this for a while. "And who are you going to meet?"

I'm not sure "just a whole lot of people from Facebook" was going to work for Mrs. Havilland.

"Just some kids from Grammar."

I could see a small nod of approval – obviously "kids from Grammar" was a good move – but I still had the sense that I needed a clincher.

My eyes fell on Mrs. Havilland's phone on the bedside table.

"Imogen can send you a text, like, every hour, telling you where she is, that's she's okay," I said.

"A text every half an hour," Mrs. Havilland said.

Every thirty minutes was ridiculous, but I said "Okay" and went upstairs to tell Imogen the good news.

"Really?" she said.

"Really," I said.

I don't think either of us could quite believe how straightforward it had been.

After reminding us of the text-every-half-hour condition and kissing her daughter good-bye, Mrs. Havilland let Imogen go.

As we walked through the door and up the path, as we went through the Halcyon Grove main gate, I kept expecting to hear Mrs. Havilland's voice calling Imogen back.

Even when we were on the bus, five kilometers up the road, I still half expected to hear it.

"Please don't leave me, you're the only thing I've got left."

But I didn't.

OVER FLOW

Town Hall Square wasn't big enough for all the people who had turned up; they were crowding the footpath, spilling out onto the road. There were uniformed police shouting through bullhorns, ordering people to stop blocking the traffic. They were even suggesting that we should all go home.

Go home? I don't think there's much chance of that, Mr. and Mrs. Plod.

There was this crazy sense of celebration; people were spontaneously hugging and high-fiving each other.

Facebook really did have a lot to answer for, I thought. And I wondered if, had it been around in Robin Hood's day, he also would've been a viral Internet sensation.

I could see the Zolt's Facebook Fan Number 94, Miranda, sitting with her friends, a circle of emo nerds.

We walked past a news crew, reporter Teresa Budd standing in front of a camera, mike in hand. She looked tiny, much tinier then she did on any of our fifty-inch plasmas.

"This is certainly the biggest crowd I've seen here since the passing of Princess Di," she said, looking meaningfully into the camera. "That these young people are celebrating the escape of a criminal has many parents concerned, however."

I watched as a muffin – mixed berry, by the look of it – flew through the air.

"Watch out!" I yelled but my warning was too late, and the muffin collected Teresa Budd on the side of the head.

Although it disintegrated on impact, becoming a puddle of crumbs – I was right: mixed berries – at Teresa's tiny feet, she wasn't happy.

"And as you have just witnessed," she said, gripping the mike harder, "this young man is certainly no role model!"

We kept moving.

"He's the reason I get up in the morning," said somebody.

"They reckon he's gone to Vanuatu," said somebody else.

"Like, this is, like, unreal," said yet another person.

Imogen's phone beeped and she checked the text.

"Okay, Tristan's over here," she said, pushing through the crowd.

Tristan was wearing a brand new *Fly Zolt Fly* T-shirt and his customary smirk.

When he saw Imogen coming towards him he threw up his arms in a sort of mock surprise and said, "Ohmigod! Did a more beautiful girl ever walk the earth?"

It was so cheesy it made a Big Pete's pizza look dairy free, but when I looked over at Imogen she was actually blushing.

Then Tristan proceeded to give her about a thousand kisses on each cheek.

After that performance, he turned to me.

He wasn't about to shake my hand and I wasn't about to shake his, so there was a standoff.

But then we both looked at Imogen and she had this sort of pleading look on her face – *Please play nicely, you two.* So we played nicely, we shook hands.

"What do you want to do, Im?" Tristan asked.

"Im?" Who had given him permission to call her Im? I was the only one who was allowed to do that.

"I just want to absorb," she said.

So that's what we did: we absorbed, sitting down on the grass while all sorts of Zolt-related activity went on around us, Imogen dutifully texting her mother every thirty minutes. It soon became apparent – to me, anyway – that, despite the *Fly Zolt*

Fly T-shirt, Tristan knew a lot less about the object of today's gathering than even I did. So I went in hard, dredging up every snippet of information I'd retained about the Zolt, passing them on to a hopefully mega-impressed Imogen.

"Hollywood is negotiating with his mother for the movie rights," I told her.

"Really?" she said.

"And Johnny –" I started but Tristan came in right over the top of me: "You know he broke into our summer house on Reverie?"

I knew it was a despicable lie to divert Imogen's attention away from me to him. Unfortunately Imogen's usually reliable bullcrap detector wasn't working, because she said, her voice strained with emotion, "He did?"

"Yeah, he stayed there for, like, a week. Ate all the canned food. Even the Spam. Hey, he actually had a go on my flight sim."

More despicable, despicable lies.

"Why didn't you tell us this before?" I said.

Tristan ignored my question, fixing his attention even more firmly on Imogen.

"There's this big charity thing at our Reverie house during the start of school vacation. Why don't you come along and see where the Zolt slept."

I had this weird feeling that although I was there, I wasn't really there. That what had once been a triangle – me, Tristan, Imogen – had collapsed into a straight line that ran between the two of them.

"Could I really?" said Imogen.

Once, in kindergarten, Imogen had gotten so excited about a Wiggles concert that she'd wet herself. Literally. Messily. That was the Imogen I was seeing now, the overexcited, liable-to-wet-herself Imogen, and I had to do something about it. I looked at my watch in the same way somebody from a TV soap would look at their watch – very conspicuously – and then said, again borrowing from the excellent acting talent on display in those shows, "Isn't it time you texted your mother again, Imogen, as she's probably getting really worried about you?"

"I can't go," said Imogen. "Mum won't let me go anywhere."

"You came here, didn't you?" said Tristan.

Imogen looked over at me, smiled and said, "Only thanks to Dom."

Silvagni scores and leaves his opposition floundering!

Tristan was quiet. It was obvious that he was thinking, and thinking hard; you could almost hear the *click click click* of the cogs turning in his head. He looked over to where somebody was playing guitar. When he looked back again, there was a smile on his face. "Then I guess my old mate Dom had better come to Reverie with us," he said.

Of course, there was absolutely no way I was going to Reverie Island. Absolutely no way I was going to give Tristan even the smallest opportunity to get with Imogen.

And I guess there were a number of ways I could've conveyed this pretty straightforward piece of information.

A simple "No, I don't want to go" would've done the job nicely. Or, if I'd wanted to make myself look less petulant in Imogen's eyes, I could've lied, said something like, "Oh, I'd love to go, I really would. But unfortunately I have an important race on."

So did I go with either of those? No, of course, I didn't.

Instead I said, "Tristan, I'd rather eat Ronny Huckstepp's feces than go to Reverie Island with you."

Ronny Huckstepp is this tiny anonymous-looking kid at school, but there's something truly rotten going on with his digestive tract. If you saw other kids running out of the bathroom, hands clamped over their mouths, you knew that Ronny Huckstepp was in there taking a dump.

Imogen gave me another play-nicely look, this one much more severe than the previous one. And Tristan clenched his fist tight, as if it was taking every bit of his willpower to stop himself from driving it into my face.

"Only kidding!" I said. "Love to go, but unfortunately I've got this really important race on."

This seemed to work – Imogen stopped giving me the look and Tristan unclenched his fist.

After a further hour of absorbing – and two text messages to Mrs. Havilland – a girl's voice joined in with the guitar, singing to the tune of Bob Dylan's "Blowing in the Wind."

"The Zolt, my Facebook friend, is dancing on the wind …

The Zolt is dancing on the wind."

Other voices joined in.

"The Zolt, my Facebook friend, is dancing on the wind …"

The three of us stayed there until the sun disappeared, and the air was full of squawking bats that roosted in the town hall eaves. Nobody had gone home. If anything, the crowd had swollen.

Maybe it's getting close to the record held by the funeral of Princess Di, I thought.

Then, as well as the squawking bats, the singing, the guitar, there was another sound, like the buzz of a bee.

The sound got louder.

"A plane," somebody said.

"It's the Zolt!" somebody shouted.

My first reaction was "Sure thing," but as the plane came into view – according to somebody

nearby it was a little Cessna 182 – I realized that they were right.

Light planes weren't permitted to fly over the city center, especially not one flying as low as this, skimming the tops of the buildings.

So it had to be the Zolt, the Facebook hero, the modern-day Robin Hood.

Everybody was on their feet, waving, cheering or, like Imogen, declaring their eternal love. As it came nearer the Cessna swooped even lower and I started to get a bit worried.

Apparently, the Zolt had never had a flying lesson in his life. Apparently, the Zolt had learned everything he knew in his bedroom, on his computer, using flight sim. And reading flight manuals he'd bought on eBay.

If you made a mistake on flight sim, a few pixels got rearranged. If he made a mistake here, half the high schools on the Coast would have empty desks tomorrow.

As the Cessna passed over us, it wagged its wings.

I was sure I could make out the Zolt in the cockpit. And I was pretty sure he had that same cheesy smile on his face. The cheering was incredible, a tsunami spreading out and up, but it was soon joined by the sound of police sirens. And another sound, the *thwocka thwocka thwocka* of a helicopter.

Imogen's phone rang.

She answered it.

"Is everything okay?" I asked when she hung up.

"It's Mum," she said. "She doesn't like to be at home by herself when it's dark. I'd better get home."

Tristan decided that he was going too, so we all took the same bus home. Even though Imogen was sitting next to me, she spent the whole time talking to Tristan across the aisle. Actually I didn't mind being de-triangled so much, because I had plenty to think about.

If the police – state and federal – couldn't catch the Zolt, if Hound de Villiers couldn't keep hold of the Zolt, then what chance did I have?

And then I felt a flush of terror – what if I couldn't do it, what if they took my leg like they took Gus's?

Tristan and I both walked Imogen to her door and she gave each of us a hug and a peck on the cheek good night. As we walked towards Tristan's house he smiled at me and said, "You know what, Dom, maybe you and me could be mates after all."

"Maybe," I said, and I actually meant it: maybe, just maybe, we could work through our differences and learn to be, if not mates, then at least civil in each other's presence.

"Like this," said Tristan, driving his fist into my solar plexus before he walked away.

I'd been winded before, but nothing like this. It was like every molecule of air had been knocked

clean out of my body. But worse, it was like he'd also knocked out my you-must-breathe-to-live response. I collapsed on the ground, every cell in my body screaming for oxygen, but I couldn't do anything about it.

I'm going to die, I thought. *At the very least I'll have permanent brain damage.*

Then my phone rang.

You're the one that I want. Uh uh uh.

What was she calling for? I wondered, and by the time I'd finished the thought I realized that I was breathing again.

I answered the phone.

"Dom, I just wanted to thank you for everything today," said Imogen.

"That's okay," I managed.

"I know you and Tristan don't really get on."

"Oh, I wouldn't say that," I wheezed as I picked myself up off the ground.

MERE ANARCHY

The next day, at school, it was assembly in the great hall. With its high vaulted ceilings, stained glass windows and rows of gleaming pews, the great hall was the sort of place you'd expect to find God hanging out. But today it was Mr. Cranbrook, the principal, who was holding forth. Standing up high on the podium, microphone in front of him, he was telling us how disappointed he was that so many Grammar students had been at Town Hall Square yesterday.

"I know what you are all thinking," he said in his over-enunciated voice. "*But, sir, it was after school. But, sir, we were not in uniform.*"

He was right: that was exactly what I was thinking. Though probably without the *sir* bit.

"Well, let me tell you something – a Grammar boy is always a Grammar boy. Twenty-four hours a

day. Seven days a week. No matter where you are or what you are wearing."

He paused to let this sink in. "If you attend this school, then you represent this school!"

Another pause.

"All of us belong to family, to community, to nation," he said. "And, yes, we have obligations to all of these. And sometimes those obligations are onerous. Sometimes they involve work. But if we were not to fulfill these obligations, if we were to ignore the rules of our family, of our community, of our nation, if we were all to behave like Mr. Zolton-Bander, the result would be chaos. I'd like to quote from a great Irish wordsmith."

Bono? U2's lead singer was the only Irish wordsmith I knew.

Mr. Cranbrook continued. "And I'm sure some of you are familiar with the work of William Butler Yeats."

Was that Bono's real name? No wonder he changed it!

Mr. Cranbrook adjusted the microphone slightly and began to recite the poem.

"Things fall apart; the center cannot hold;
Mere anarchy is loosed upon the world,
The blood-dimmed tide is loosed, and everywhere
The ceremony of innocence is drowned."

Another pause from Mr. Cranbrook, before he gathered himself up again and said, “Gentlemen, Otto Zolton-Bander is no hero.”

I walked out of the great hall with Charles Bonthron and Bevan Milne.

“That really was an excellent speech,” I said, figuring that if I talked the talk – the Zolt needs catching – it would somehow be easier to walk the walk – i.e., catch the Zolt.

Both Charles and Bevan Milne gave me a funny look.

“I mean, Cranbrook’s right: the Zolt is no hero. He needs to be caught and rehabilitated.”

“If the cops catch him,” said Bevan Milne, “they’ll break every freaking bone in his freaking body.”

“Sorry?” I said.

“I said, if the cops catch him, they’ll break every freaking bone in his freaking body.”

Bevan Milne may have been a bit of a turd, but he was absolutely right about this. The Zolt, supposedly, was always taunting the cops online, saying how useless they were, how they would never catch him.

I was kidding myself if I thought that this installment didn’t have the mother of all deadlines: I had to get the Zolt before somebody else – the cops, Hound de Villiers, some reckless vigilante – did.

At lunchtime I went immediately to the library. Mr. Kotzur was on duty. He rode a recumbent bicycle to school and was vice president of the Gold Coast Stars Wars Society

"Mr. Silvagni, to what do we owe this unexpected pleasure?" he said.

I wouldn't say I'm exactly a regular at the library, especially not during lunchtime when I'm more likely to be found at the basketball court shooting baskets or on the field kicking a ball around, but I didn't think there was any need for Mr. Kotzur to go the sarcastic route with me.

For a second I considered returning a bit of what I'd just gotten, say something like, "I've just come in to bask in the glow of your incredibleness," but I didn't: in a library it's the librarian who's got all the power.

So instead I said, "I'd like to use a computer, sir. I left my laptop at home."

"Did you book?" he said.

"I didn't think I had to," I said.

"You don't!" said the librarian. "Got you a beauty. You should've seen the look on your face. Priceless! Hop onto number eighteen, stormtrooper."

I hopped onto number eighteen and logged on to Facebook.

Well, tried to log on to Facebook, because it was blocked. I'd forgotten about the school's Net Nanny, or whatever it was called.

I sent a text to Miranda telling her the problem.

Yes, Miranda – like me – was at school. Yes, she – like me – wasn't supposed to have her phone on. Yes, she – like me – wasn't supposed to send texts.

It took less than a minute to get a reply from her, a step-by-step explanation on how to trash Net Nanny.

I followed the instructions and it worked a treat – I was able to log on to Facebook.

I'd assumed that the Zolt, Facebook hero and all, would have his own page: the Zolt posting messages poking fun at the cops; the Zolt offering tips on how to eat well while maintaining a fugitive lifestyle. But I was disappointed.

There was an Otto Zolton-Bander page, but it was a fan page, created by somebody else.

He did have 1,421,356 fans, though.

Make that 1,421,357 fans.

1,421,358 fans.

Okay, put it this way: he had a rapidly expanding fan base.

And an incredible number of postings, especially since he'd escaped. As you'd expect, there were plenty of people who loved the Zolt, who posted stuff like:

Keep it going, Zolt.

and

Fly, Zolt, fly.

But there were also quite a few people who

hated him, and it became evident from looking at the page that when you hated the Zolt, it became your life's work.

Zolt you are skum and when they catch you they will throw you in jale forever you skum.

It also became evident that when you really hated the Zolt, you couldn't spell very well either.

There was also quite a lot of stuff for sale on the website. *Fly Zolt Fly* T-shirts (hand-screened) for $24.95 (s&h not included). *Fly Zolt Fly* coffee mugs at $9.95. Bumper stickers ($4.95). Mouse pads ($3.95). There was a song called "The Ballad of the Zolt" that you could download from iTunes for $2.95.

As I scrolled through the posts, I had this weird feeling that I wasn't the only one looking at this material. I looked around the library, which was now pretty much full, and saw the librarian's reflection in the window. He was sitting at the desk, gazing at a screen, but every now and then he'd sneak a look at me.

Is it him? Is he monitoring me?

One way to find out.

I brought up Google.

Typed in *star wars sucks*.

There were about a million *Star Wars* hate sites. I clicked on the most venomous-looking one. A video started playing, a spoof of the famous "I am your father" scene.

Immediately the reflected librarian had a look of shock and outrage on his reflected face.

It was him!

I logged off immediately and left the library, returning the librarian's if-looks-could-kill glare with a grateful smile. Without knowing it he'd taught me a lesson: Be careful, stormtrooper, because you never know who in the universe is watching you.

SNIFFING OUT THE HOUND

After school I hurried home; at least there, in my bedroom, on my computer, on my network, there was much less chance of being cyber-snooped.

It didn't take me very long to realize that I had to find Hound de Villiers, PI.

Because, let's face it, the local cops hadn't been able to track down the Zolt. Neither had the Queensland police. Not even the television networks had been able to find him. There was only person who'd done that. And even though he'd ended up, according to some reports, floating around the harbor naked and handcuffed to his boat, that didn't take away from the fact that he, and he alone, had managed to find the Zolt.

Finding him wasn't actually that difficult, because Hound de Villiers, PI, had a considerable web presence. From his Wikipedia entry I learned that he'd been born Hansie de Villiers in Cape Town in South Africa and had served "with distinction" in the South African Army, attaining the rank of lieutenant. That he'd worked as a mercenary in a number of conflicts in Africa and South America. That he'd settled in San Diego in 1984 and had subsequently worked as a bounty hunter. That he'd left the USA two years ago under mysterious circumstances and moved to Australia, setting up business on the Gold Coast. I also learned that he'd been married three times, had seven children, and in his spare time enjoyed hunting pigs and reading the novels of Matthew Reilly. Further investigation revealed that he worked for a company called Coast Surveillance.

I called them.

"Hello, my name is Dom Silvagni and I'd like to talk to Mr. de Villiers if I could, please."

"Rack off, kid!" said the less-than-polite man at the other end before hanging up.

Houston, we have a problem. And that problem was: me. More specifically, my lack of adult status. Not only did I look like a kid, I sounded like one too. Unfortunately, kids aren't always taken seriously, especially not in the very non-kidlike world of private investigating.

I spent about an hour on Google researching voice modulators, devices attached to your phone

that changed your voice so you could sound like somebody else. Donald Duck. Darth Vader. Even Darth Duck. Or, in my case, an adult. But then I suddenly realized that I was wasting my time.

Hound de Villiers had been a mercenary: he'd risked his life for money. Hound de Villiers was now a PI. Was he driven by a sense of social justice, a need to put bad guys behind bars? Maybe, but I didn't think so. It must be the money. I had to look at myself differently. I wasn't just a fifteen-year-old kid, I was a fifteen-year-old kid who had money. Money that Hound de Villiers wanted.

I composed an email: *I would like to purchase an hour of Mr. de Villiers's time. How much?*

And sent it to the email address on the Coast Surveillance website.

It took only half an hour to get a reply.

$400 cash.

I felt both excited – my plan had worked – and outraged – four hundred dollars for an hour, who did he think he was?

I composed a reply.

Okay. When?

And got one back immediately.

Tomorrow. Ten. Bring cash.

Tomorrow at ten I had school, but I wasn't going to tell him that: I was an entity with money, not a schoolkid.

My email: *Can we make it 4, instead?*

Their email: *Okay. But cost is $500.*

Five hundred! If I was outraged before, I was outraged to the power of two now! But I also felt like a bit of a sucker – I should've questioned the four hundred dollars, not just accepted it like that. Too late, though.

Okay, I wrote, and hit send.

So that was it: tomorrow at four I was meeting Hound de Villiers, the only person in the whole of the country who'd managed to track down the Zolt.

All I had to do now was get five hundred bucks. Here was the irony: my parents were filthy rich, and to them five hundred dollars was nothing. If I went to them and said: "Could I have five hundred dollars to pay renowned private investigator Hound de Villiers for an hour of his time in order to help me catch the notorious fugitive Otto Zolton-Bander and so avoid losing my leg," then they'd give it to me.

But I couldn't. Cardinal rule of The Debt: no help allowed. I logged into my savings account: I only had two hundred dollars.

I hesitated, then I knocked on the door to Toby's room.

Once upon a time, and it did seem like a fairy tale ago, my little brother and I had been pretty good mates.

We'd played together, gotten into trouble together, but then something had happened. It hadn't been anything major, we'd just sort of drifted apart.

And I think we'd both decided that we didn't like each other, so those were the roles we played now.

I knocked and said, "Tobes, it's me."

"Rack off," came the voice from inside.

See what I mean?

"Don't be like that," I said, opening the door.

Most kids Toby's age would have posters of movie stars, sports stars, rock stars on their walls. Toby had chefs. Heston Blumenthal. Ferran Adrià. The one with the potty mouth. They were all up there.

As for Toby, he was on his computer, looking at porn.

His sort of porn, anyway.

A photo of a naked, voluptuous … orange cake.

Gastronomic porn.

"Wow, that looks so delicious," I said. "You going to make it?"

"I thought I told you to rack off," he said.

"Wow!" I said, quickly scanning the recipe. "So you actually boil an orange for a whole hour. That's pretty wild."

Toby looked at me, and I knew this whole thing was in the balance, that he could go either way.

Eventually, when he said, "It is wild!" I knew I'd managed to pull it off.

We discussed the cake for quite a while longer, and I have to admit, it actually was quite interesting. For example, the cake had no flour – only something called almond meal.

Eventually, when I thought the moment was right, when some of that uncomplicated brotherly affection we used to freely bestow on each other when we were little had been restored, I said, "Toby, how would you feel about lending me three hundred dollars?"

I knew Toby had money in the bank, and plenty of it. I knew this because I saw it come in – pocket money, birthday and Christmas presents – but I didn't see it go out. You see, if I needed some new running shoes, I had to pay for them. But if Toby wanted something – a new mixing bowl, a new, improved type of whisk – he was able to persuade Mom that she was the one who needed it and she'd end up shelling out for it.

"You want me to lend you three hundred?" said Toby.

"That's right," I said.

Toby pondered this for a while before he said in an American accent, "Okay, I'll lend you three C but the vig's twenty."

"The vig?"

"Didn't you ever watch *The Sopranos*? The vig, the juice."

"You mean the interest?"

Toby nodded. "The vig."

"So I pay you back three twenty?"

Toby scoffed at that, and Toby, like Miranda, did good scoff.

"Twenty percent, not twenty dollars!"

Twenty percent was outrageous, but I didn't have any choice.

We shook hands, Toby logged into his account and transferred the money into mine.

As I left his room it was with a mixture of feelings: I was relieved that I'd managed to procure the money I'd needed, but I was also aware that my own brother had just ripped me off. Still, what choice had I had?

SNIFFING WITH THE HOUND

After school the next day I made my way past the bus stops and out onto the main road. I put out my hand to hail a taxi and one appeared within seconds.

"Where we going today?" the driver said with an accent.

He was older than Dad, younger than Gus, with olive skin and a bushy gray moustache.

I glanced at his license on the windshield. Under a faded photo was the name Luiz Antonio DaSilva.

Was he Spanish? I wondered. Or Portuguese?

"The Block," I said.

"The Block is no place for a nice kid like you."

"I'll be fine," I said, though I wasn't too sure that I would be – the Block had a reputation as the roughest, toughest area in the whole Gold Coast.

Luiz Antonio shook his head.

"I come from the streets of Rio, I know what these places are like," he said. "The people take one look at you and think *carne fresca*."

"*Carne fresca?*"

"Fresh meat," he said.

"The address is 542 Russell Street," I said.

He practically exploded.

"Russell Street! You've got to be kidding me! What you want to go there for? You're not trying to score drugs or anything, are you?"

"No, nothing like that," I said. "I have a meeting with a private investigator."

"Yeah, well, plenty of them on Russell Street. And do you know why? Because the place is dirty with criminal scum. Come on, let me take you back home."

"You can do that if you like," I said, "but I'll just get another taxi who will do what taxis are supposed to do and drop me off at my requested destination."

Luiz Antonio thought about this for a while before he said, "What number was it again?"

"Five forty-two."

It didn't take long to get to the Block, only about fifteen minutes, but it really was a long way from Halcyon Grove.

Dad had said that when he was a kid the Block had been the place to hang out, their version of Robina Mall. But now most of the shops were boarded up and the few people on the streets didn't look like they were the shopping types.

We pulled up outside a run-down building, two-stories, with Cash Converters on the bottom floor and the words *Coast Surveillance* in faded gold lettering on the double-paned window upstairs. When I went to pay, Luiz Antonio said, "We can settle at the end."

"This is the end."

"No, it isn't," he said. "You're my passenger, you're my responsibility. I'm staying here until you come out. Besides, you think it's easy to catch a taxi in this area? Take it from me, it isn't."

"Suit yourself," I said, thinking he was being overdramatic.

There were people loitering outside the Cash Converters, mostly men, mostly smoking. At first I thought this was cool, like I'd walked into a movie, the badass scene with all the badass guys. It didn't take me long to change my mind, however. Not after a man in a red bandana who was blocking the entrance made no effort to move, even though it was pretty obvious that I wanted to go in. Now I was doubly aware of the five hundred dollars in my pocket, of what I must've looked like to him: "fresh meat," to use Luiz Antonio's phrase. I looked at my watch. It was already four, time for my appointment.

"Excuse me," I said, appalled at how puny my voice sounded.

The man didn't move.

A horn sounded.

Luiz Antonio, leaning across, yelled through the window, "Hey, bro, let the kid through, can you? He's hocking his mother's wedding ring so his old man can have some drinking money."

There was a murmur of approval – it was every son's duty to hock his mother's wedding ring so his old man could have some drinking money.

I went straight upstairs to find two people waiting inside the Coast Surveillance office. They had that same bored, frustrated look that people have in the emergency room of hospitals.

"I have a meeting with Mr. de Villiers," I said to the bulgy woman behind the counter.

She consulted a computer screen.

"You're Mr. Silvagni?" she said.

"That's right," I said. "My meeting's at four."

"Wait a moment, can you?" she said, before she picked up a phone and said something softly into the receiver.

Eventually she put the receiver down and said, "And you brought the cash?"

"That's right," I said, keeping my voice down.

"Okay, down that corridor, second door on the left."

I knocked on the door and got a gruff "Enter" as a response.

Hound de Villiers's office was much less shabby than the building had suggested. The floor was carpeted and the walls were covered in framed photos. Immediately I was reminded of Gus's office. These weren't photos of runners, though; these were photos of one man: Hound de Villiers.

And they all seemed to be a variation of the same theme: Hound de Villiers in a bicep-baring T-shirt holding – fondling? – a large gun. I'd already deduced one fact about Hound de Villiers: he liked money. A lot. But I was pretty sure I now had another fact to add: Hound de Villiers liked Hound de Villiers. A lot.

Although the version of Hound de Villiers sitting behind an expansive desk was older than the one in the photos – his features were craggier, his long blond hair was thinner – it was unmistakably him. He was wearing another bicep-baring T-shirt and I noticed, under the desk, faded jeans and cowboy boots.

"Sit down," he said, waving at a chair.

I did as he asked.

"The money?" he said.

I took the wad from my pocket and handed it over to him. He counted it, thumbing through the bills with practiced ease.

"Okay, what do you want?" he said.

"I want to talk about the Zolt."

At the mention of that name, there was a dramatic, almost theatrical, change in his expression. I had a

third fact to add to my rapidly expanding list: Hound de Villiers hated the Zolt.

Hated him as much as those people on Facebook who hated him hated him.

"He a friend of yours, is he?" he said, his eyes boring great smoking holes in me. Immediately I needed to get out of there. I didn't care about the five hundred dollars, I just needed to get out, to do what I did best: run like the wind.

Hound de Villiers was scary. Very, very scary.

And when he stood up, I almost crapped myself. I knew from his Wikipedia entry that he was six foot three, but there's six foot three and there's six foot three.

I mean, the Obi-Wan-Kenobi-loving librarian was probably six three, but who was scared of him?

This six foot three, however, could snap off my head.

This six foot three could squash me like a cockroach.

"When all else fails," Gus always says, "you gotta find your form. Form is the bedrock."

I took his advice and tried to find my form: relaxing my shoulders, slowing my breathing, I said, articulating carefully, "No, he's definitely no friend of mine."

All six foot three of head-snapping, cockroach-squashing Hound de Villiers sat back down.

And I did some quick thinking.

The first thing I knew about Hound de Villiers was that Hound de Villiers liked money. But unfortunately Hound de Villiers already had my money.

The second thing I knew about Hound de Villiers was that Hound de Villiers liked Hound de Villiers. A lot.

If the government ever passed same-sex marriage and then moved on to same-person marriage, I reckon he'd be the first one up.

Do you, Hound de Villiers, take Hound de Villiers as your legally wedded spouse?

Ya!

You may now kiss yourself.

"Mr. de Villiers?" I said.

"The name's Hound," he said.

"Hound, I was just wondering why nobody else could find him but you could."

"Cops," he said dismissively. "Cops think like cops, they can't help themselves. But when you're dealing with a punk, you've gotta think like a punk." His accent was all over the place: part South African, part American, with a touch of fair-dinkum Aussie.

I felt like I should be taking notes: *When dealing with punk, think like punk.*

"He's a smart punk, I'll give him that, but he's got something else going for him, something much more valuable."

Virtual pencil poised to make another note, I waited for Hound de Villiers to tell me what this was, but he didn't.

Instead he looked at me and said, "You got some balls on you, kid."

I responded to this compliment with a little shrug of my shoulders.

"Hey, but that probably comes with the territory, eh? Old man as rich as yours. Probably think you're bulletproof. Probably think that money's going to get you out of any trouble you get into."

He knows who I am!

"Don't look so surprised, I like to do some research on my clients. Besides, your dad and me, we've got history."

My dad and Hound de Villiers – surely not. He was making this up.

"You done your research on our punk, Dom?"

"Just what I've read online."

"Then you know his old man died when he was eight? His stepfather took off when he was eleven? You know that after that he spent more time with foster parents than with his useless mother?"

I nodded. Yes, I knew all that. Except the "useless" bit.

"So what do you reckon that's done to him?"

"I guess he probably doesn't trust many people."

"You're dead right: the punk doesn't trust anybody.

And that's his greatest asset. Because if you're on the run, the less people you trust, the better."

Again I felt like I should be taking notes: *If on the run, the less people you trust, the better.*

Hound de Villiers leaned back in his chair, his hands clasped behind his head, and said, "You know how I catch most fugitives?"

"By tracking them down?"

Hound de Villiers unclasped his hands and shook his head.

"Because people talk, that's how."

Hound de Villiers looked at his watch.

"Well, it looks like our time's up," he said.

It was four-twenty!

"But how did you find him when nobody else could?" I said, trying to appeal to his vanity again.

"Cops," he said dismissively again. "It's all there, under their noses, and they're too stupid to see it."

"It's all where?"

"Facebook," he said. "Now get out of here."

I didn't need to be told twice. I got up, walked across to the door.

"Oh yeah, and one more thing."

I turned around. "What's that?"

"The next time I catch your friend – and don't worry, I will catch him – I'm going to kill him."

My eyes flickered over all those photos of Hound de Villiers with his biceps and his guns, and I had no

doubt that he was serious, that he'd killed before, and that if he caught Otto Zolton-Bander, he was going to kill him too. Which was exactly why I had to get to the Zolt first.

Outside, the taxi had gone.

The man in the red bandana approached me.

"Let's start with the watch," he said.

There was no malice in his voice, just a sort of matter-of-factness. I was *carne fresca*, he was a meat-eater; this was how the world worked.

I thought about taking off, and I had no doubt I could outrun him – he looked too big, muscle-bound – but where could I run to? I knew nothing about the Block, or this side of the city for that matter. I'd started unclipping my watch when a hand grabbed me by the elbow.

Carne fresca, I thought. *Of course, they're going to fight over it.*

"Let's go."

It was Luiz Antonio.

"Don't look behind," he whispered. "Just keep walking."

I did as he said until we reached the parked taxi. We got inside, he started the engine, swung the wheel hard and we took off with a squeal of rubber.

CREATURES OF THE NIGHT

It had seemed like a good idea to go back to the Block that very night. "Cloak of darkness" and all that.

Especially since Mom and Dad had gone to some big charity function and Gus was "looking after" us.

It didn't take me long, however, to realize that it wasn't a good idea at all. Because at night the night creatures come out. They huddle on the corners, they skulk in the shadows, their hooded eyes watching your every move. Though technically they aren't vampires, or werewolves, they have exactly the same desires: to drain your blood, to feast on your flesh.

And this taxi driver, unlike Luiz Antonio, didn't hang around, didn't even question what I was doing. He just took my money and got out of there.

I walked past the Cash Converters. Although there was a light on, the front door was locked and there was no movement inside.

"Hey!"

From the shadows, a voice.

"What?" I said.

"You want some, kid?"

"No," I said, hurrying on.

At the end of the block I turned right, and walked quickly until I came to the service alley I'd seen on Google Maps. I hesitated. At least on the street there were streetlights, but down here the gloom was only occasionally relieved by the weak light spilling out from barred windows. I had to keep going, however. This was my plan, and I needed to stick to it. As for my backup plan, it was pretty basic: run like Usain Bolt, and keep running like Usain Bolt.

I walked hesitantly down the alley, past the overflowing trash cans, the scurrying rats, the stench of garbage filling my nostrils, until I came to the back of Cash Converters. I took a quick look around before I started climbing up the fire escape. It was loose, and each step resulted in a loud rattling noise, a noise that I was certain the whole neighborhood could hear. Nobody came, nobody called out, so I kept climbing, stopping at the second floor.

I tried the door. As I'd expected, it was locked. I took the tension wrench out of my pocket, inserted it partway into the lock and turned it as far as it would go. I took the pick out and got to work. Earlier, when I'd picked all the locks in our house, it'd had been surprisingly easy. There was nothing easy about this, though. Especially as I was halfway up a fire escape, in the most dangerous part of the city. Still, the first pin was straightforward. So was the second. The third pin didn't want to go, though. I remembered what it said in the lock-picking manual I'd downloaded from the Internet: *Project your senses into the lock to receive a full picture of how it is responding to your manipulations.* At the time it'd seemed a bit, well, Zen, but now it was all I had so I projected away, trying to imagine the troublesome third pin.

It must be a modified, I thought. Perhaps a mushroom pin.

I recalled what the manual said about mushroom pins: less torque on the wrench, more pressure on the pick. I put this into action and it worked – I was able to set the pin. The fourth and fifth pins were also straightforward.

I gently pushed the door open and the alarm went off.

According to my research I had twenty seconds until the base was contacted.

Down the corridor, down the stairs and into the Cash Converters. I grabbed the phone line and ripped it out of the wall. The alarm was still going, but I was hoping that wasn't an issue. Even in good neighborhoods people had alarm fatigue; I really didn't think anybody around here would care less. I figured that as long as the security company hadn't been alerted, I was fine.

Back up the stairs, and the door to Hound de Villiers's office wasn't locked. I turned on the light. When I recognized a Garmin Oregon 550 in the top drawer of his desk I knew that it was the answer to my break-and-enter dreams. It was a handheld sat nav and a camera.

I could've just taken it, I suppose.

But somehow that seemed too much like stealing, and I may have technically been a criminal but I was certainly no thief. I turned it on and scrolled through the photos, stopping at the photo that had been on the television, in the papers: the Zolt handcuffed to a tree.

And, being a sat nav, it gave the latitude and longitude, the exact place the photo was taken. I copied these numbers into my iPhone, smiling as I did. Espionage? Piece of cake.

"What's so funny, snot nose?"

I looked up. At two night creatures: a vampire, a werewolf. Ready to drain my blood. Feast on my flesh.

The vampire brought a knife up high so I could see it. The size of it. The seriousness of it.

"I said, what's so funny, snot nose?"

How stupid was I to assume that everybody would ignore the alarm, that there were no concerned citizens? Of course, they were concerned, concerned that they wouldn't get part of the spoils.

"Here, it's all yours, fellas," I said, holding out the sat nav.

The vampire swiped it from my hand.

"Where's the money?" demanded the werewolf.

"What money?" I said.

The vampire flashed the knife.

Thup!

A drop of blood hit the floor.

I looked down. My hand was bleeding. Now that I could see it, I could feel it too, the steady throb of blood leaving my body.

"I don't know," I said, panicked by the blood. "I don't know anything about money."

"The money," said the vampire, coming closer.

Middle distance running is often about gaps, about finding a way between two bodies. My hand reached down and grabbed a handful of paper, tossing it in the air. The two creatures were momentarily distracted and I took off, running between them. Again the knife flashed, the tip catching my shirt, but I was through. Out of the door, down the corridor. Back out through the fire escape door. I could hear them, but they had no chance. A mere vampire, a mere werewolf, against an elite runner. I clambered down the fire escape stairs into the alley. Just as I was about to take off, a third night creature appeared

out of the gloom and grabbed me. Wrapped his arms around me. Squeezed me.

"He's got all the money," yelled the vampire from the fire escape.

My arms were pinned, but my hand managed to reach into my pocket and grab the pick. I jabbed it down hard into the night creature's arm. It punctured flesh, but I maintained the pressure, feeling it travel deeper and deeper, until it hit something hard.

The night creature screamed, released his grip.

And I ran.

And kept on running until the Block and its creatures were far behind me.

A $9.99 CASIO KEYBOARD

"The Jazys have asked us over," Mom said to Dad at breakfast the next day.

Dad looked up from the *Financial Review* and did this sort of pouty thing with his mouth.

"Not the crumby Jazys," said Toby.

"That's so, like, you know, like," said Miranda, mimicking Briony's precocious way of talking.

Both my siblings looked at me, no doubt expecting my usual excellent anti-Jazy contribution.

"Yes, let's go to the Jazys' house!" I said, almost American in my enthusiasm. "I'd love to spend some quality time with Tristan."

Of course, they all thought I was being ironic, or facetious, or whatever the word is, so I had to keep enthusing, take it beyond ironic, or facetious, or whatever the word is.

"No, seriously, Tristan's a really nice kid," I said, recalling the really nice punch in the guts.

"Yeah, right," said Miranda. "Once you get past all that obnoxiousness."

"All that obnoxiousness probably comes from a place of deep insecurity," said Mom, who'd obviously been watching *Oprah* lately.

"Absolutely," I said. "A place of very deep insecurity."

I'm not sure whether it was my enthusiasm that did it or not, but we ended up at the Jazys' house, dipping crackers into dips, listening to Mr. Jazy talk about real estate.

Mr. Jazy was a short, thickset man whose most distinctive feature was a black, bushy beard that seemed to go from his neck to just below his eyeballs.

"Prices in the Gold Coast can't keep going up," he said. "The bubble is going to burst any day now."

Dad didn't agree, however.

"There is no bubble," he said. "As long as people from down south keep moving up here, then demand will outstrip supply and prices will keep trending upwards."

"Look at the stats, Dave. They're not the ones driving this. It's people who already live here, re-mortgaging, buying rental properties. Really, it's one huge Ponzi scheme."

I was looking right at Dad when Mr. Jazy said this and a look passed across his face.

It was almost like he'd been caught out.

It didn't last, though, and Dad quickly returned to his usual good-natured self.

"Ponzi schemes?" he said, half laughing. "You really do come out with some rippers."

"Why don't you kids go and play?" said Mom, who obviously thought the conversation was getting a bit too Ponzi for our ears.

"You want to play Xbox, or something?" I asked Tristan as we went outside.

"Why are you being so freaking nice?" he said. "It's creeping me out."

Not as much as it's creeping me out, I thought.

But again I remembered those coordinates from the photo on the Hound's Garmin Oregon 550. How every time I entered them into Google Earth they came up with the same location: Gunbolt Bay on Reverie Island.

Still, Tristan was right: nice wasn't the way to go with somebody like him.

"So this summer house of yours?" I said.

"What about it?"

"I don't think it's as big as you reckon it is."

"Not as big as your summer house, you mean?"

"Nowhere near it," I said.

"You're a moron," said Tristan.

“Prove it,” I said.

“Prove that you’re a moron?”

“No, that your summer house is bigger than ours.”

“Yeah, right,” said Tristan. “You want us to bring them both here so we can compare them?”

Occasionally, like now, when you looked at Tristan, you didn’t see anything but smirk. No legs, no arms, no torso; just a disembodied smirk.

“Or I could check it out myself. Take you up on that offer and go there with you, it’s school vacation after all,” I said.

“You said that you’d rather eat Ronny Huckstepp’s feces than go to Reverie Island with me,” he said.

I’d hoped he wouldn’t bring that up.

“It’s just a figure of speech,” I said, but Tristan didn’t look convinced. “As if anybody would even contemplate eating Ronny Huckstepp’s feces.”

Tristan considered this for a while. “We’re leaving tomorrow.”

“I’ll have to ask Mom,” I said.

Tristan looked at me, and there was an expression on his face that I didn’t get: was he grateful, or surprised, was he even going to cry?

Right then I got the tiniest glimpse of Mom’s theorized place of deep insecurity. It was only the tiniest of glimpses, and it didn’t last long, but for a moment it made me wonder whether I had misjudged Tristan.

"And you'll sort it with Imogen, of course."

"Imogen?"

"Yeah, Imogen," he said, hand moving to his crotch. "That's the only reason I invited you in the first place, dipstick."

"Okay, I'll sort it," I said. Nope, I hadn't misjudged him; Tristan Jazy was *so* not okay. I had no idea how I was going to persuade Mrs. Havilland that she should let her precious daughter go away, but I wasn't going to tell him that.

Tristan gave me a playful punch on the shoulder – playful for him – before he said, "Silvagni, you're going to wish you ate Ronny Huckstepp's business when you see how big our house is."

And then he disappeared inside to, as he put it, "hang with the serious people."

I knew that it was no use, that there was no way I'd ever get Imogen away from her mother, but I called her anyway.

"Thanks so much for saying yes," she said immediately.

"Sorry?"

"I know you don't really get on with Tristan and I really appreciate it."

Again, all I could come up with was, "Sorry?"

Imogen explained it all to me.

How Mrs. Jazy had kept calling Mrs. Havilland, asking her if Imogen could come to Reverie Island

with them. How there was this charity barbecue on. How Mrs. Havilland had kept saying no. But then Mrs. Havilland's sister had decided to come to stay during that weekend. Because she wouldn't be alone Mrs. Havilland had finally relented and said yes, but on one proviso: that Dom go along, too. Sensible, responsible Dom. That it wasn't just Tristan and Imogen.

"So we're going," Imogen said, excitement lifting her voice several octaves.

"It seems like it," I said.

It was exactly what I wanted, what I needed for The Debt, but why did I have this feeling that Tristan has just played me like a $9.99 Casio keyboard?

POSTCARD WORTHY

It was a three-hour trip to where we'd catch the ferry to Reverie Island. Mr. and Mrs. Jazy took turns to drive the 8-seater Lexus, while Tristan and Briony took turns to whine.

"I don't know why we didn't take the plane," whined Briony from the very back seat where she sat next to Imogen.

"Cars are so boring," whined Tristan from the middle seat where he sat next to me.

It was soon obvious why Mr. Jazy and his extensive facial hair liked to drive, though.

"Those places are already returning low eights," he said, pointing to some newly built houses that seemed to have sprouted overnight like mushrooms. "Kicking myself I didn't get a piece of that."

He seemed to know the value of every building we passed; it really was pretty incredible. Occasionally

Mrs. Jazy would look up from her Sudoku and say something like, "Well, you have enough on your plate already, dear" or "There's only twenty-four hours in a day, dear."

When we stopped at a small town for a bathroom stop, Mr. Jazy said, "This joint has to be the next to move."

I looked around. It was a pretty place with little weatherboard cottages with rosebushes out in front. Two old men were sitting at a table in a nearby park playing chess.

"It just can't stay like this, can it?" said Mr. Jazy, looking at me.

"Why not?" I said.

"Too close to the sea, and that new highway's being built. This place has got to move. And soon."

One of the old men picked up a piece, went to move it, but changed his mind and put it back again.

I remembered what Mr. Jazy had said to my dad yesterday.

"So what's a Ponzi scheme?" I asked.

Mr. Jazy smiled at me, the same way a teacher smiles at you when you ask them a question about their pet topic.

"It's an investment scheme where the returns are paid from other investors' money, not from any actual profits."

I must have looked a bit blank, because he went

on to explain it further. When he'd finished I said, "What happens to Ponzi schemes in the end?"

"They run out of gas," he said. "They run out of new money and things get ugly."

"How ugly?" I said, wondering if this could possibly happen in the Gold Coast.

"You're talking money, son. Lot and lots of money. So the answer's real ugly. Things get real ugly."

Surely Dad was right, I thought. Surely things couldn't get real ugly somewhere like the Gold Coast.

"So you're interested in real estate?" Mr. Jazy asked me, scratching at his beard.

"A bit," I said.

"Well, it'd have to be more than his nibs over there," he said, indicating Tristan who was touching his toes, showing Imogen how flexible his hamstrings were. "Don't know what's the use of building up a business when there's nobody to take it over."

"Total bummer," I said.

Mr. Jazy gave me a funny look. "So you and Tristan are really hitting it off, eh?" he said as we walked back to the car.

"Totally," I said, trying to manufacture some enthusiasm.

"Well, you're going to love Reverie," he said. "Plenty of mischief for a couple of likely lads to get into."

After another hour of driving we took the ferry from the mainland to Port Reverie, the main settlement on the island. While the Jazys went to the supermarket to buy supplies, I managed to persuade Imogen to go for a walk.

What was once a bank was now the Bank Café.

What was once the Post Office was now the Post Office Café.

The whole place, it seemed, had been café-fied.

"It's such a pretty little town," said Imogen.

"I'll think you'll find that technically it's a village," I said.

"What's the difference?"

"Villages go on postcards, towns don't," I said.

Okay, it probably wasn't the funniest joke I'd ever made, but it did exactly what it was meant to do; it made Imogen laugh. And I doubted whether Tristan's hamstrings, no matter how flexible they were, could ever do that.

We stopped in front of a lamppost.

Taped to one side there was a poster advertising the Island All-Comers Mile Race, which was taking place next Saturday.

And taped to the other side was a wanted poster. Concerned Citizens of Reverie Island (CCORI) was now offering a reward of thirty thousand dollars for information leading to the apprehension of Otto Zolton-Bander. Under his photo, the one taken by Hound de Villiers, was his description: *Male Caucasian, 6' 5", with blue eyes, dark hair and fair complexion.*

Imogen took a photo of the poster with her iPhone.

"Imagine, he could be just around the corner," she said.

I loved to see Imogen excited like this, but I just wished it was about something else. Like me, for example.

She was absolutely right – he could be just around the corner, because something told me that Otto Zolton-Bander had returned to this island.

That was not what I wanted other people to think, though. The last thing I needed was an island full of trigger-happy rednecks looking for a trophy.

So yesterday when I'd read a report on the Internet that a gas station attendant in Bundaberg was certain that he had served the Zolt, I'd known exactly what I had to do. I'd spent hour after hour posting this dubious piece of news in blogs, forums, e-zines. I tweeted it, I texted it, I Facebooked it.

And I knew I'd succeeded when Miranda had later said, "The Zolt's in Bundaberg."

"How do you know that?" I'd asked.

"It's all over the net."

On the way back to the supermarket to meet the Jazys, Imogen and I stopped at a gift shop so she

could buy a few of those village-inspired postcards. And she wasn't one of those people who could just grab the first few on the rack. No, she had to analyze every single one, make sure it met her exacting requirements.

While she did this, I had a look around the shop. There was the usual crap, including some *Fly Zolt Fly* T-shirts. But what caught my eye was another T-shirt that said, *We didn't find Yamashita's Treasure but we still found Gold on Reverie!*

The phrase *Yamashita's Treasure* sounded vaguely familiar but I wasn't sure how.

"What exactly is Yamashita's Treasure?" I asked the shop assistant as she walked past.

"Don't ask me, I'm from the mainland," she said.

But an old man who was standing nearby said, "It was the treasure looted from Asia by the Japanese Army occupying the Philippines during the Second World War."

"But what's it got to do with Reverie Island?" I said.

"Well, there is one theory that somehow after the war a ship carrying the treasure ended up in this area."

"Sounds pretty far-fetched," I said.

The old man smiled at me and said, "Stranger things have happened," before he walked away.

By now Imogen had bought the best three

postcards in the shop and we walked back to the supermarket.

As soon as we left town and headed inland the landscape changed dramatically. There wasn't much you'd want to put on a postcard here, that you'd want to turn into a café. The land was scrubby with the occasional prefab house set up on blocks. There were rusted-out vehicles, busted lawn furniture, and mongrel dogs that barked at the passing cars. For the first time on the whole drive Mr. Jazy was quiet. I knew that the Zolt had been brought up in this area, and his mother and his younger sister still lived here.

"There was a vibrant community here in the seventies," said Mrs. Jazy. "I'm afraid this is all that's left."

"Somebody should drop a bomb on them," said Tristan.

"Or poison their water," said sweet little Briony.

Which set the Jazy children off on ways to rid Reverie Island of its less successful residents.

Until Mrs. Jazy said, "Kids, that's enough!"

By that time we were almost on the other side of the island and the landscape had become postcard-worthy again. Especially with the sun setting so spectacularly and the low clouds shot through with an array of extravagant colors.

Mr. Jazy had found his voice again. "That place in there," he said, pointing to an enormous stone wall, "was sold last week for eight point four. Had my chance, too, a few years ago when it was on the market."

"You really do have enough on your plate, dear," said Mrs. Jazy.

By the time we got to the Jazys' summer house it was dark. Beyond a high wall was … an enormous, rambling two-story edifice. Immediately Imogen wanted to be shown where the Zolt had allegedly slept. It looked like a pretty normal bed to me, but to Imogen it was some sort of sacred site. She took photos with her phone. She knelt down next to it, eyes closed. And when Tristan suggested that she could lie on the bed she went into this crazy "me not worthy" routine.

Like I said before, you didn't have to be any sort of pysch-anything to understand why Imogen adored the Zolt – him free, her not, that sort of thing – but her behavior was starting to get pretty annoying.

I could see, too, that despite everything, Tristan was no Zolt worshipper either. And suddenly I had a glimpse of the solution to a problem that had been bothering me ever since I'd agreed to come here.

I didn't see how I could find the Zolt without Tristan's help. He knew this area, he had access to a boat. But – cardinal rule of The Debt – I couldn't ask

Tristan to help me find the Zolt.

But what if – and this was the mother of all what-ifs – it was Tristan who asked *me* to help *him* find the Zolt?

"And to think the Zolt's probably still on the island somewhere," I said, momentarily buying into Imogen's Zolt-love.

Tristan wasn't happy with this, though: "No way he's still on the island."

"Way," I said. "In fact, I reckon I have a fair idea where he is."

I knew exactly what Tristan was thinking: *You, you pathetic dude, are just trying to impress Imogen.* But I also had the sense that I'd planted a seed.

"Hey, Imogen," Tristan said, "let's watch a movie."

I immediately agreed. "Let's."

I got the thermonuclear look from Tristan – it was Imogen he wanted to get into a dark room, not me – but I wasn't going to give up that easily. So it ended up with the three of us in the cinema. And if you think cinema's an exaggeration, that's because you haven't been to the Jazys' summer house.

It had THX, it had Dolby, it had Surround Screen. And Tristan had managed to get a copy of a Zipser Brothers movie that hadn't even been released yet. I wasn't sure it had even been made yet.

I could see why he would do that: he, like me, knew that Imogen was a big Zipser Brothers fan.

What he didn't know but I did was that Imogen was a discerning Zipser Brothers fan; she only liked the fifty percent of Zipser Brothers films that were any good. And this one – thank God – wasn't one of those. In fact, it was terrible, and I could see that Imogen, despite THX, Dolby and Surround Screen, was quickly losing interest.

So I took a punt and said, "You know what, I'm really tired. I might go to bed."

And, remembering this thing I'd read once about yawning being contagious, I followed this statement with several prodigious yawns. It was a big risk, because if Imogen didn't follow my lead then I'd have no choice but to de-triangle, to leave the two of them alone in this dark room. Imogen and the Crotchgrabber.

But she did!

"Yeah, I might hit the sack, too," she said, standing up.

Tristan had pile-drived me in the guts once, and if Imogen hadn't been there I was quite sure he would've visited some more ultraviolence on my person, but she was there, so he couldn't do anything except seethe.

He was still seething when Mrs. Jazy gave Imogen and me the choice of three bedrooms: the Goa Room, the Bali Room or the Morocco Room.

"Do you mind if I have the Morocco Room?"

I asked Imogen.

"Hicham El Guerrouj?" she said.

I nodded. As far as I knew, no runner from Bali or Goa had broken as many world records as he had.

Tristan was still seething when I said good night. Still seething when I saw Imogen to the door of the Bali Room.

And as I got into my Moroccan bed, got between Moroccan sheets, got ready to have Moroccan dreams of winning Olympic gold, I knew that he was still out there, seething. So I got out of bed and made sure the door was locked.

LIKE WOW! HIDEOUT

I woke early, intending to go for a run, which would also serve nicely as a reconnoiter of the area.

I picked up my iPhone but then put it down again – I sometimes preferred to run without it bouncing around in my pocket.

When I descended the stairs, Tristan was lying in wait for me. And waiting was the right word – there was something predatory about the way he was crouched there at the bottom of the stairs, ready to pounce.

"Let's go for a spin in the boat," he said.

I didn't like the way his eyes were glinting, but I did like the idea of a spin in the boat because, as far as I could work out, that was the only way you could get to Gunbolt Bay.

"Let's," I said.

We followed the path down to the pier, where a

sail boat, a metallic-red ski boat and various kayaks were tied up.

My eyes followed the island's shoreline as it folded continually back on itself, forming a series of bays and inlets.

"Do you reckon your loser father could afford something like this?" Tristan asked as he retrieved a key from its hiding place and we got into the speedboat, which had outboards that looked disproportionally large.

"Probably not," I said, though now that I'd been to the Jazy summer house I knew that ours was, in fact, bigger.

Tristan untied the ropes and turned the ignition. The monster outboards kicked into life, the whole boat vibrating.

Tristan put it into reverse, and when we were clear of the pier, he suddenly jammed his foot on the accelerator. The outboards roared, the boat lifted up, and I went flying backwards. If I hadn't managed to grab a handhold, I would've ended up in the water.

Tristan laughed and the thought crossed my mind that he wanted to kill me.

Of course, it was a crazy thought, a ridiculous thought.

Wasn't it? When I thought about it, though, this was an ideal opportunity: two boys and an

overpowered speedboat was an accident waiting to happen.

For a second I thought about aborting the mission, telling Tristan I wanted to go back, but this was too good an opportunity – I had to keep going. Besides, I could imagine only too vividly Tristan's reaction if I told him I wanted to go back: he'd never let me forget that one.

I don't think you can be a runner and not love speed, even speed like this that was totally dependent on the consumption of mega-liters of fossil fuel.

Wind in my face, I couldn't help smiling as the speedboat skimmed across the water's surface.

We followed the coastline, passing houses that seemed to get bigger and grander as we went. And Tristan, it appeared, knew who owned every one of them.

"That's Cameron Jamison's property," he said, pointing to a gleaming white mansion. "He was number eighty-seven in this year's BRW rich list."

Maybe Mr. Jazy had Tristan all wrong; maybe his nibs would end up in the same business as his father after all. Just without all that facial hair.

There were no more houses now, just rain forest that tumbled down to the water.

"Imogen's pretty crazy about the Zolt, isn't she?" I said. "It's like she thinks he's invincible or something."

Tristan thought about this for a while. “So you seriously reckon you know where he is?”

“I’ve got a fair idea,” I said.

“How come?” he said, which was a pretty fair question: I mean, why would I, Dominic Silvagni, have a clue where the Zolt was when nobody else did?

“I’ve done some research,” I said.

“How come?” he said, and again it was a pretty fair question.

I took out the folded wanted poster and handed it to him.

“So what?” he said.

“Thirty grand? You call that ‘so what?’” I said.

“I thought you Silvagnis were supposed to be rolling in it.”

“We are rolling in it,” I said, because there was no use denying that. “But that’s my parents’ money, not mine.”

Tristan handed me back the wanted poster and I thought that was it, I’d have to find another way to get where I needed to go.

But then he said, “Okay, if we collar him, you can keep the money. But I’m the one who gets to bring him in, okay?”

“Okay,” I agreed.

“So where we headed?”

“Gunbolt Bay,” I said.

“That’s miles away,” he said.

"What, there's not enough fuel to get us there?"

"Enough fuel in this bad boy to go to New Zealand if we wanted," he said. "Let's go!"

Of course, it occurred to me that Tristan had another very good reason to go so far from home. If that accident-waiting-to-happen did happen, then it would be easier to explain away.

If we'd been going fast before, we were flying now; the boat's hull didn't even seem to be touching the surface of the water. We only passed a couple of boats: a fishing trawler with its boons extended, and a yacht, its sails hanging limply.

Tristan seemed to know what he was doing, but I couldn't help wondering what would happen if we hit something like a submerged log at this speed. How many times the boat would catapult in the air. How mangled our bodies would be. How much the sharks would enjoy their unexpected meal.

So, despite my speed-love, it was actually a bit of a relief when he eased his foot from the accelerator.

"That's it over there," he said, pointing towards an arc of sand between two rocky headlands. "What should we do?"

"Let's go and have a look," I said.

Tristan raised the outboards and we drifted into the beach.

"Okay, throw out the anchor," said Tristan.

I did as he said.

Tristan took the key from the ignition and put it back into its hiding place. We got out of the boat and waded through knee-high water to the shore.

It was so quiet, just the wash of the water on the sand, the swish of the wind in the trees.

What if the Zolt was here? And what if, as the police seemed to think, he was heavily armed?

We were – quack quack – sitting ducks.

As soon as I had that thought I felt sort of ashamed of myself. After all my research, I felt as though I'd gotten to know Otto Zolton-Bander pretty well. Yes, he stole planes. And boats. And cars. And DVD players. And Xboxes. And mobile phones. And iPods. Okay, he'd stolen a whole lot of stuff. But he'd never hurt anybody.

Like most people on his Facebook page I didn't believe he was heavily armed. And even if he was, he would never shoot two defenseless kids.

No, it wasn't the Zolt I should be worried about, it was Tristan.

He could pile-drive me in the guts, even bash my brains in with a rock, and nobody would know.

"Come on, let's do this thing!" said Tristan, adopting a crouching fighter's pose, karate chopping the air a few times.

"Let's do this thing" was without doubt my least favorite phrase in the world, but I sensed now that we were close to the Zolt's lair.

"Okay," I said. "Let's do this thing."

We did this thing, walking from one end of the beach to the other, but we couldn't see any tracks, any way into the thick rain forest.

"Nice one, Silvagni," said Tristan. "You wouldn't last one episode of *Survivor*."

The phrase from the lock-picking manual came to mind: *Project your senses into the lock to receive a full picture of how it is responding to your manipulations.*

Okay, I wasn't picking a lock, but the theory was sort of the same – stop looking at this place with your eyes, look at it with somebody else's – namely the Zolt's.

There was no way somebody as clever as the Zolt, somebody who had eluded capture like he had, was going to signpost where his hideout was.

I did another inspection of the beach, trying to look at it through the Zolt's eyes.

"You're wasting our time," said Tristan, kicking at the sand.

But I wasn't: on the eastern headland there were worn-looking patches on the rocks that tumbled out of the rain forest.

I started climbing, following these up, and it was soon obvious that they corresponded to footholds and handholds.

I really had to stretch to reach some of them,

though. But then I remembered – the Zolt was six foot five!

"This way!" I yelled at Tristan.

He followed me as I scrambled up through the rain forest.

"Out of my way!" he said a little while later, and I had no choice but to stop and let him pass. Eventually I reached a level path that followed the line of an escarpment.

"What took you so long?" said Tristan.

No waves, no wind – it was even quieter here, and the only sound was the crunch of leaf litter under our shoes. After five minutes of walking, we found ourselves in a small clearing.

"Well?" said Tristan. "Is this it?"

I recalled the photo of the Zolt handcuffed to a tree. Behind him had been a rock.

My eyes scanned the escarpment, the jumble of rocks at its base. Again, I could see smooth patches.

"This way," I said, following these as they led me up over a small rise.

Again Tristan scrambled past me, and he was the first one down into the hideaway of Otto Zolton-Bander.

"Wow!" he said.

"Wow!" I agreed.

Wow! Wow! And more wow!

This was without doubt the most wow-worthy place I'd ever seen. The escarpment wall tilted forward, forming a natural shelter. In its shade was a ring of blackened stones, cooking utensils, cans of food, a chair fashioned from logs. Beyond that was the entrance to a cave.

I followed Tristan inside.

I noticed the fissures in the rock above, through which light entered. There was a foam mattress with a sleeping bag. A chair that had been fashioned out of driftwood. A desk that was an upturned shipping crate. On which was a pile of maps.

"He's well gone from here," said Tristan, and I was pretty sure he was right: the hideout had an abandoned air about it.

I flicked through the maps and immediately realized I was wrong about at least one thing: they were charts, not maps, because they were of coastal areas.

Some of these charts were old, their paper soft, pliant, while others were much newer, their paper stiffer; but they had one thing in common: they were of this general area.

I opened out one of the older maps.

There were pencil marks all over it, but particularly on the blue areas, the sea. Some of these marks were numbers but others were weird hieroglyphics.

"This is like a diary or something," said Tristan.

I looked up to see that he was reading a small notebook.

On TV, when the cops are on somebody's trail, the clues are always scarce: a discarded cigarette butt, a piece of paper with a phone number scrawled onto it, but this was Clue Central.

And I wasn't quite sure what to do with it all. I folded the map back up and put it on the top of the pile. As I did I noticed that it had a name written on it in faint pen: *Dane G. Zolton*.

"Wow, this cave keeps going," said Tristan, his voice echoing.

Looking up, I said, "What are you doing back there?"

"I gotta pee."

"Go outside then!"

As Tristan went outside, I picked up the notebook he'd been reading.

Opened it.

There was a noise from outside, the sound of a gun going off. Tristan appeared, his eyes wide with terror, his shorts wet with terror.

"It's the Zolt, he tried to shoot me!"

"Did you see him?" I asked.

"He's got a gun!"

Another noise. Again, a gun going off.

"This way," I said, shoving the notebook into my pocket, moving deeper into the cave.

The cave quickly became a tunnel and we had to crawl on hands and knees.

"What if it's a dead end?" came Tristan's strained voice from behind me.

I'd thought the same thing, but I couldn't believe that somebody as smart as the Zolt wouldn't have an escape route. Everything else about his hideaway was so perfect – surely there wouldn't be only one way in and out.

"It's still going," I said to Tristan as I scraped my head on the top of the tunnel.

Dropping onto my stomach I continued crawling, commando style.

"I'm going back!" said Tristan.

"Don't be crazy," I said. "This is the way out."

But was it the way out? It was pitch-black now and the panic came at me in waves. When I started to feel myself losing control, I did what I'd been taught in running: breathed in deeply, tried to rein in my galloping thoughts.

You've been diagnosed as coimetrophobic, not claustrophobic, I assured myself. *You're scared of cemeteries, not confined spaces.*

When I noticed a pinprick of light ahead, I said nothing. But when that pinprick got bigger I said, "I can see the exit."

"Thank God!" said Tristan.

Thank the Zolt, I thought.

I crawled out into the blinding sunlight and onto a ledge ten meters above the water, and only big enough for two people to stand on.

"Be careful," I said as Tristan followed me onto the ledge.

When he realized where we were, something crossed his face. Was it fear? But it was only a flash and then it was gone and Tristan's normal expression returned.

"Don't be such a wuss," he said.

Maybe this was the extent of the Zolt's planning, as far as his escape route went.

I didn't believe this, however. I peered over the edge, looking for a way off the ledge. The cliff face was smooth, though; not even a sticky-fingered rock climber could get across that.

"Can you go back into the tunnel for a sec?" I asked Tristan. "I need some room to get down on my stomach."

He did as I asked and I crawled back into the tunnel. Then, legs spread-eagled, I edged my head further and further over the precipice.

A flash of red, of plastic.

"There's a kayak down there," I said as I carefully got to my feet. I knew the Zolt wouldn't just leave us up here.

"But how do we get to it?" Tristan asked as he carefully edged back onto the ledge.

"I reckon you've got two choices: either you jump or you dive."

"That's really funny, Silvagni."

"Is it?" I turned around, took a small step and jumped off the cliff.

I'm glad I was wearing shoes, because my feet hit the surface hard, and then I was going down, the momentum taking me deeper and deeper. The water was cool and clear; down below I could see a bed of kelp, fronds waving at me, welcoming me.

I was going too deep, I was starting to run out of air, so I kicked hard with my legs, reached up to grab handfuls of water. It worked and I started ascending, eventually breaking the surface, gulping in air.

High on the cliff I could see the ledge, Tristan looking over. I waved at him and he jumped. He landed a meter or so away from me; the splash was tremendous. When he surfaced, and got some air back into his lungs, he actually smiled at me.

"That was mad!" he said.

We untied the kayak from where it was tethered to a tree root. Removed the paddle that was jammed between the root and the cliff.

Although it was a single, we both managed to get on board. Tristan sat right at the stern, and I shuffled back until I was wedged between his legs.

"Steady on, Silvagni!" he said.

I wasn't so keen to get this close to Tristan either. Because getting close to Tristan usually meant pain. But I'd mucked around on kayaks enough to know that unless you got all the weight back, they were very difficult to maneuver.

I started paddling.

We quickly decided that we had to go back to the boat, that there was no way we could paddle this kayak home. I kept as close to the cliff as possible. We rounded a corner and Gunbolt Bay came into view. Our boat was exactly where we'd left it. But there was another speedboat there as well. Blue, bigger than ours.

"That must be his," whispered Tristan.

Another dip of the paddle and the other headland, the one we'd climbed, came into view. A man was sitting on the beach, facing away from the water. In his hands was a rifle. Even from there I recognized him: it was the man with the red bandana who'd blocked the entrance to Cash Converters the day I met with Hound de Villiers.

"Is that him?" whispered Tristan. "Is that the Zolt?"

"No," I said.

I'm a runner, not a swimmer, but Coach Sheeds – unlike Gus – believes strongly in cross-training, so we spend quite a few hours each week in the pool.

I backed the kayak out of view again.

"I'm going to swim and get the boat," I said.

"He'll shoot you," said Tristan.

"He's not expecting somebody to approach from the sea," I said. "He's totally focused on the track."

"He'll shoot you," said Tristan again.

"I'll meet you back here," I said.

"He'll shoot you," said Tristan.

I slid off the kayak and started breaststroking, making as little splash as possible. The beach came into view. The man hadn't moved; his gaze, and his gun, was trained on the rocks of the headland. Slipping through the water, I approached the boat.

Voices from the beach.

"It's me."

"Okay, gun down."

"Still in there."

"Why don't you smoke him out?"

"Might have to."

When I got close enough to the boat, I took a lungful of air and duck-dived. Now I wished I didn't have shoes on: they felt cumbersome and weighty as I made for the bottom. I saw the taut anchor line and followed it down. My fingers fumbled as I tried to undo the knot.

If only I had a knife, I thought.

But I didn't.

Fingers fumbled.

Lungs burned.

The knot loosened.

Pain behind my eyes.

I pushed the end of the rope through, and again. Once more and the rope was untied. I wrapped it tight around my hand, and made for the surface.

Once there, I sucked in air. With each lungful the pain in my head lessened.

If I tried to get on board here, if I started the motor, he'd just pick me off with the gun.

I started swimming away, pulling the boat along behind me. Luckily for me, it slipped easily across the surface of the water.

I was out of sight of the beach. One more tug and the boat would be out of sight too, and I could climb on board.

Then that sound again – the report of a gun – and a bullet zinged across the surface of the water.

This wasn't a computer game, this wasn't an action movie; this was a real bullet and it had just missed me! I wanted to be outraged, or astonished, but I didn't have the time, so instead I yanked at the rope.

Another report, another bullet. But I was out of sight now so I hoisted myself on board, retrieved the key from its hiding place, slotted it into the ignition, turned it. The outboards sputtered, then roared into life.

I rammed it into forward and pressed down hard on the accelerator. The motors roared but the boat didn't move.

Crap! The outboards were up.

But which button was it?

"The red button!" came a voice over the water.

Tristan was paddling frantically towards me.

Which red button?

A distant roar of an engine – the other boat had started up.

The kayak smashed into the side of the boat and Tristan scrambled on board, into the driver's seat. He hit a button and the outboards lowered. He pressed down on the accelerator. The boat reared up like a wild horse, leveled and took off.

The other boat was behind us. We were flying, we were rocketing, and it didn't seem possible that they could be gaining on us. But they were, and it almost felt as if there was something supernatural about them, as if they weren't bound by the laws of nature. I could make out three figures in the boat, two of them holding guns.

"I can't go any faster," Tristan said. "Their boat is bigger and more powerful than this one."

Should we just stop? Show them who we were? Show them that we weren't Otto Zolton-Bander?

Tristan's eyes were on the sat nav.

"There," he said, pointing to something.

He swung the wheel and we were heading for the shore. I wondered what his plan was: ram the boat into the shore and try to escape on foot?

Bad plan, Tristan, I thought. They'd just pick us off with their guns.

But then I saw it, a break in the low-lying shore. A creek.

"I went kayaking there a few months ago," he explained. "And it's pretty shallow."

Now I got it.

"Too shallow for them?"

"That's the plan."

Tristan eased his foot slightly from the accelerator when we entered the creek, but with the trees whooshing past, so close I could've leaned out and touched them, it felt like we were going twenty times faster than we had been before.

That stuff I said about runners loving speed? Okay, I take it back. All of it.

I looked behind. The boat was still there, still gaining. One of the figures had his gun raised, pointed at us. Tristan's eyes were on the echo sounder.

The needle was rising quickly, the water becoming shallower: *3 meters, 2 meters, 1 meter, .5 meters*.

The propellers hit the bottom and the boat slewed to one side, the water churning into a muddy brown color. They soon found water again, though, and we took off.

I looked behind. The boat had dropped back. The plan had worked.

The distant report of a gun.

We both ducked but there was no whistle of a bullet.

Already they were too far away to cause us any harm.

The creek opened out and we were back in the bay again.

"Well done," I said, slapping Tristan on the back again.

Tristan returned the gesture, but when he'd finished slapping he grabbed a handful of my wet shirt and yanked it hard, causing me to topple over the side and into the water.

SHOT

Like I said before, I'm an elite runner but far from an elite swimmer. Still, I have a fair lung capacity, so when Tristan turned the speedboat around and came at me, its knifelike bow cutting through the water, I sucked as much air as I could into my fair lung capacity and waited until the very last second before I went deep.

I still couldn't quite believe it: Tristan was actually trying to kill me. I could hear the high-pitched whine of the motor, feel the churn of the blades above me. I waited until they had faded before I surfaced.

Tristan and the red speedboat were two meters away.

He'd tricked me, he'd cut the motor.

"Come on," he said. "Get in."

"You tried to kill me!" I said.

"Don't be so over-the-top, I was just mucking around," he said.

Really?

Then a gun went off and Tristan went down, his head hitting the ski pole before he sprawled face-down on the boat's backseat. On the far bank I could see the man in the red bandana, rifle raised. I swam over to the boat, hoisted myself on board.

"Tristan? Are you okay, Tristan?"

In reply, a moan.

Blood was pouring out of him, over the seat, pooling in the boat's hull.

Another report, and a bullet whizzed over our heads. Keeping low, I crawled to the boat's bow. Reaching up, I turned on the ignition.

The motors roared into life.

Another bullet whizzed over me. One hand on the bottom of the steering wheel, one hand pressing down on the accelerator, I lifted my head up to sneak a look and swung the boat around until it was heading in the right direction.

More zinging bullets.

And more moaning from Tristan.

When there were no more bullets, I carefully raised my head higher and looked behind. I couldn't see Red Bandana, but I still waited for a while longer before I sat up.

"Tristan, you okay?"

"They shot me," he said. "They shot me."

I took off my T-shirt and used it to wipe the blood from Tristan's face. Soon, it became obvious what had happened: he'd nicked his cheek on the ski pole as he'd collapsed.

"Am I going to die?" he said.

"Probably," I said.

"I can't die now! I can't!" said Tristan.

I wanted to watch him suffer a bit longer – payback for pushing me off the boat – but I couldn't, it was just too ugly.

"You didn't actually get shot," I told him.

It occurred to me that if they had wanted to kill us we'd both be dead by now. This wasn't shoot to kill, this was shoot to scare.

"Where do you think all this blood is coming from, you moron?"

He did have a point – there was a lot of blood for such a small nick: head wounds are like that – but eventually I was able to convince Tristan that he hadn't been shot, that he didn't have any holes in his body that hadn't been there when he was born.

The blood eventually stopped flowing and what was already on the boat was easy to wash off.

When we pulled into the pier, Imogen was waiting for us, sitting cross-legged on the edge. Her hair was loose and the breeze was moving it around her face. She looked like somebody out of an ad for something pure and wholesome. And I wanted to cry. Whether it was because she looked so beautiful, or because we'd just been shot at, I wasn't sure, but

there were some mega-emotions swirling around in my body.

"Where have you two been?" she said.

I looked over at Tristan, at the divot of skin missing from his cheek, splotches of blood on his clothes.

"Mucking about in boats," I said.

Tristan put his hand up to his cheek.

"What happened to you?" Imogen asked, her voice full of concern.

"He fell on a rock," I said.

"Tristan?" said Imogen.

"I fell on a rock," he said flatly.

Imogen didn't look convinced. "On the boat?"

"We landed," I said. "Checked out this really cool island. And Tristan slipped and fell. It's nothing really. Just a graze. Isn't that right, mate?" My eyes searching Tristan's, I said, "It's a miracle he didn't break anything, actually."

He opened his mouth and I thought that was it, he was going to say "I almost got shot!" but instead he said, "It was a miracle."

Mr. and Mrs. Jazy were having a late breakfast outside and we had to go through the same charade with them.

This time, thankfully, Tristan's performance was more believable. And though Mrs. Jazy was a bit concerned, Mr. Jazy wasn't.

"Boys will be boys, eh?" he said, rummaging around in his beard.

"Come on, let's take the Merc for a spin," he said to his son. "I need to visit the caterers, make sure everything's okay for tomorrow."

Great, I thought. Now I could sneak off to my room, check out the notebook that was still in my pocket. I was worried that it would be wrecked and all that work – locating the Zolt's lair, getting shot at – would be for zilch.

But Imogen cornered me as I made for the stairs.

"What really happened?" she demanded, a very un-Imogen-like tone to her voice.

"Like I told –"

"You're a terrible liar, Dom," she said. "Did you do something else to him?"

"To him?" I said, and now I was starting to get angry.

Me do something else to him?

What about his pile-drive to the guts? What about him trying to run me over in the boat?

"Yeah, I tried to kill him. Because then I'd have you all to myself."

As soon as these crazy words left my mouth, I wanted them back. They were way too close to the truth.

"Very funny, Dom," Imogen said. Then she stormed off.

FLOWERS TOO OTTO'S DEAD

I took the notebook out of the pocket of my shorts. Sodden, its pages were stuck together. I thought of all the clues we'd had, how smug I'd been – Clue Central, I'd called it – and now all I had was this mess. I used the Moroccan hairdryer in the Moroccan bathroom to carefully dry it out. Then I tried to separate the pages but with frustratingly little success. After two hours of effort all I got was a scrap of writing. Though the ink had run, it was still legible.

flowers too otto's dead

Legible, but it didn't make much sense. Still, something about it was naggingly familiar. I brought up Facebook on my iPhone.

The Zolt's fan page.

He now had 1,466,253 fans.

I started scanning the posts, screen after screen

of them. Over and over and over again until my eyes began to hurt.

Ten more screens, I told myself. *Ten more screens and I'll go back downstairs*. On the eighth screen I found that exact line, in a posting by somebody called Tailspin.

> not the easiest friend
>
> must go real love
>
> flowers too otto's dead

This posting had been "liked" by one person with the Facebook name "Hera." Obviously, it was some sort of love poem to the Zolt.

And the line, so weird on that scrap of paper, didn't look so weird anymore. Poetry, love or otherwise, was not exactly my area of expertise and I didn't really have a clue what the poem was about.

But then it occurred to me: how could it be a love poem to the Zolt when he was the one who had written it – the last line, anyway?

So Tailspin had to be the Zolt, I reasoned.

And Hera must be the person he was communicating with. The "like" was their way of acknowledging the post. By why use Facebook to communicate?

It took me a while to work out the answer to that, but when I did it made perfect sense: because all the other usual means of communication – mail, phone, email – were being monitored by the police.

But who was Hera?

A quick Google and I had one answer: Hera was the mother of the gods. From that answer I deduced another answer: Hera was the Zolt's mother, it had to be.

Now I could see how brilliant their method was: even if the police were monitoring her computer, there was nothing suspicious about viewing her son's Facebook fan page, hitting the occasional "like" button.

But what exactly was the Zolt saying to his mother?

I kept reading the poem, over and over again, trying to work this out.

After a while, my brain started to faze, my eyes started to unfocus and the poem lost what little meaning it had and became just a soup of letters.

And this was the best thing that could've happened to me, because I realized that I'd been concentrating on the really obvious way to arrange letters, on the words.

But what if there was another, less obvious, arrangement? Some sort of hidden code?

I decided to concentrate on the phrase in the notebook: *flowers too otto's dead*

I got a pencil and wrote *f*, the first letter of *flowers*, on a piece of paper. Then I focused on *too*, the second word.

ft didn't make sense, so I wrote *o* next to *f*; I now had *fo*.

Moving on to *otto's*, I had three choices *foo, fot* or *fos*.

Now *dead,* the last word.

Using *foo* I tried all the letters – *food, fooe, fooa,* and again, *food.* Using *fot* I got *fotd, fote, fota.* Using *fos* I got *fosd, fose, fosa.*

Given the Zolt's predicament, holed away like that, *food* seemed very promising.

Now when I took the phrase and underlined those letters – *flowers too otto's dead* – I could see a definite pattern: first letter in word, last letter in next word, first letter, last letter, and so on.

Could it really be that simple? Excitement mounting, I put my theory to the test, underlining the appropriate letters in the rest of the poem.

not the easiest friend

must go real love

It wasn't a love poem, after all. It was a pretty simple message: *need more food.*

To say I was excited by this revelation was an understatement – this was the first big break I'd had.

And what's more, I'd worked it out by myself.

Suddenly, catching the Zolt by the end of the month didn't seem so impossible after all. I'd already decided that tomorrow I would go and pay Hera, the Zolt's mother, a social call.

CONFIDENT HAIR

Again, I woke early. Again, I put on my running gear. Despite having congratulated myself several times on not taking my phone yesterday – it would've gotten very very wet – I decided to take it along today. This morning there was nobody downstairs, no crouching predator, and I managed to escape the house. As I punched the security code into the front gates, a truck pulled in, with *Reverie Caterers* written on the side. Today was the Jazys' charity barbecue.

Gus had not been happy that I'd come to Reverie and last night he'd sent me a text: *don't forget your training!*

So I set the timer on my watch to forty minutes and took off along the side of the road towards town. It was such a beautiful place to run that for a while there I actually managed to forget about all my troubles. But then the timer on my watch buzzed, the forty-minute run was over and it was time to get back to work.

I wasn't what you would call an expert hitchhiker but there were no buses, no Lexuses, so I didn't have any choice. I stuck out my thumb and the first car that came along stopped. It was some car too. A Ferrari.

"Where you off to?" the driver asked.

He was about my dad's age. Wore the same sort of designer shades. Rolex on his wrist. Same confident hair.

"Into the town," I said.

"You're in luck," he said. "Get in."

I went to get in, but there was a pile of books on the front passenger seat.

The man, noticing my hesitation, said, "Just put them on the floor."

I did as he said, got in, buckled up, and he took off. Immediately, I could tell he was a very good driver. That the Ferrari wasn't wasted on him.

"This is a really nice car," I said.

He looked across at me. And smiled.

His face wasn't smooth like my dad's face, not straight like my dad's face.

This was a face that had taken a few.

"So you're staying with the Jazys," he said.

"That's right," I said, though I didn't think he was actually asking a question. "Do you know them?"

"We all know each other this side of the island," he said.

It was then that I noticed the title of the book

sitting on the top of the pile: *Gold Warriors: America's Secret Recovery of Yamashita's Gold*.

I pointed at the book. "An old bloke in the shop yesterday was telling me about Yamashita's Gold. Is that a good book?"

"It's rubbish," he said, and the way he said "rubbish," it was like the book itself was a pile of festering putridness.

"Why?" I said.

"Because it is," he said.

Obviously this wasn't his favorite topic of conversation, because he changed the subject. "That you in the speedboat with young Tristan yesterday?"

"That's right," I said.

Was he what's-his-name? I asked myself. Number 87 on the BRW list?

"You kids out shooting, were you? I heard a few shots."

"No, there were these rednecks," I said.

"Rednecks?" He paused, and for a second I thought he was going to come out with something insightful about rednecks, but he left it at that.

A Mazda was dawdling in front of us. Because the road wound this way and that, we couldn't pass.

"I should've taken the chopper," he said.

"You've got a chopper?"

Even my dad didn't have a chopper.

"Sure, used to have a nice little plane, too, until

Mr. Zolton-Bander decided to bang it up."

The mention of the Zolt so casually like this was like an electric shock running up my spine. I wasn't sure why. Reverie Island had a small population. The Zolt was an industrious criminal. Sooner or later I was bound to meet one of his victims.

"So where do you think he is?" I asked. "Still on the island?"

The road ahead straightened out. He put his foot down, the Ferrari growled, and we ripped past the Mazda.

"No, I don't think that's possible," said BRW Number 87. "What takes you to town, anyway?"

"Umm. A latte," I said, thinking of all the cafés I'd seen in town earlier. "The Jazys' machine is just not pulling good shots. And I'm, like, this latte freak."

"I'm hearing you," he said, and he gave me a long explanation as to where to get the best latte in town.

When we got there, he insisted on taking me to the café in question and buying me one, and an apple danish to go with it. I noticed that they had a *Zoltocino* on the menu – a double shot with a hit of guarana, *guaranteed to keep you on the run*.

As we sat there, people kept coming up to our table to say hello to him.

"You sure know a lot of people," I said.

"I was born and bred on the island," he said.

After we'd finished our lattes, BRW Number 87

said, "Tell you what, I've only got a few bits and pieces to pick up in town, why don't I give you a ride back?"

"Thanks," I said, "but I'm really keen to have a look at … at the architecture in the village."

"You're interested in architecture?"

"Can't get enough of it."

"Look, if you do decide you want a lift, here's my card. I'll be around town for the next hour or so."

"Thanks," I said, taking the card. "And thanks for the latte."

Cameron Jamison, it said.

Just as I'd thought: it was him. BRW Number 87.

I walked back through town, past a shop window full of the Zolt merchandise. The place was crowded with shoppers, all keen to get themselves a little piece of the Zolt.

As I walked inside I heard one woman say, "I'll have five T-shirts. My relatives in the States are desperate for them."

I picked up a *Run Zolt Run* coffee mug and turned it over. Made by RBY Enterprises. I checked the label in a T-shirt. Made by RBY Enterprises.

"Can I help you?" asked the assistant.

"These mugs are cool," I said.

"We also have a new model that has just come in," she said, handing me a mug with *The Zolt Is No Mug!* written on the side.

I checked underneath. RBY Enterprises again.

"Wonder what will happen if he gets caught?" I said.

"I guess all this stuff goes back to the warehouse," said the assistant. "And my boss stops walking around with that great big smile on his face."

I was pretty sure that her boss wasn't a member of the CCORI then.

"So you want that?" she asked.

"No –" I started, but I changed my mind. "Sure, and can you gift wrap it for me?"

"Certainly," said the assistant.

Present in hand, I walked quickly through town and out onto the road. When I heard a car approaching I turned around to check it out. It was a black Hummer, not the Ferrari, so I put my thumb out.

The Hummer stopped.

The window slid down.

"Get in," said the driver.

"Perhaps not," I said.

But Hound's telescopic arm reached out and Hound's enormous hand grabbed a handful of my shirt and Hound yanked me through the window and inside the Hummer.

"Buckle up, punk," he said. "You and me are going for a drive."

When, a couple of minutes later, we turned off the main road, onto a rutted dirt track, and into what

looked like the town's unofficial dump, my anxiety levels started to soar even further. There were rusted car bodies and old mattresses and piles of festering garbage. It was the sort of place where a little extra garbage, like an adolescent's body, wouldn't be noticed. Hound turned off the engine. Looked at me with his mercenary's eyes.

Then said, "Where's my sat nav?"

"What sat nav?" I said, feigning innocence.

Except you don't get to feign innocence with somebody like Hound.

He stared at me harder, his eyes unflinching, and said, "You broke into my office, you little —"

"But I didn't take your sat nav," I said.

And then I got it, the chain of cause and effect: the vampire had hocked the sat nav to Red Bandana, Red Bandana had worked out it was Hound's sat nav, had found the photo of the Zolt, had formed himself a posse in order to bring the Zolt in and claim the reward money.

"The man with the red bandana's got it," I said.

Hound chewed on this piece of information for a while, then he said, "Look, I reckon you and me, we're after the same thing. Not sure what your motivation is – rich kid like you doesn't need the money. Don't really care. But what I'm proposing is that instead of treading all over each other's toes, we pool our resources."

"But you want to kill him," I said.

"Of course I don't want to kill him. That was just to scare you. Hey, I've got three ex-wives and seven kids to support; I need that reward money."

I didn't know whether or not to believe him. To somebody like my dad, thirty grand wasn't that much money. But to somebody like Hound, maybe it was.

"So tell me what you know," he said.

I had to give Hound something, I knew that. Otherwise I was in danger of becoming garbage. "I know that he communicates with somebody using Facebook," I said. "His user name is Tailspin."

Hound smiled at me.

"You're a smart operator. Tell you what, you ever get sick of being a snotty-nosed rich kid, I'll give you a job."

I suddenly found myself thinking of that line from Shakespeare that my English teacher, Mr. McFarlane, was always trotting out: *He flatters to deceive*.

"So how did you find that out?" he said.

"I went through all the postings on the Facebook page," I said. "Over and over again, and there were some that started to look suspicious."

Hound nodded.

"Once I'd zeroed in on those, it was easy as to crack the code. It was pretty simple," I said, allowing myself a touch of arrogance.

"Technically it's a concealment not a code, but,

hey, I'm loving your work. Okay, so tell me this, boy wonder: who was he communicating with?"

I was just about to say, "His mum, of course," but I stopped myself.

"Pool our resources" he'd said, but so far he hadn't done much pooling.

"So how come you let him get away?" I said.

The color rose in his face. His hands gripped the steering wheel, his knuckles turning white. Hound, obviously, had anger-management issues and for a second he looked like he was going to lose it.

He managed to restrain himself, however. "Fair question," he said. "I was taking him across to the mainland in a boat. Had him cuffed, there was no way he could get away."

"But he did," I said.

"The boat appeared out of nowhere. Guns everywhere. ASIO types on board. Telling me that the kid's a national security risk, and that they can't let me land him. 'Of course, you'll get your reward,' they tell me. 'You're a national hero,' they tell me. So I let them have him."

"They weren't ASIO?"

"Of course they weren't," he said. "Oldest trick in the book, and I fell for it."

He really did seem to be disgusted with himself and I felt sorry for him.

"Hey, everybody has an off day," I said.

"Not in this game, you can't," said Hound. "Too many off days and you're a corpse."

"And the Nutella?" I asked.

"The Nutella is bullcrap. You hear that? Bullcrap. Some idiot puts rubbish like that on the Internet and next thing you know it's spread all around the world."

I couldn't help laughing. Hound's enormous hand wrapped around my neck, squeezing.

Like I said, anger-management issues.

"What's so funny?"

"Nutella, spread all around the world. I thought you were making a joke," I said, forcing the words through a constricted esophagus.

Hound de Villiers relaxed his grip.

"I don't make jokes. You got that? Never."

"Got it," I said.

"Okay, so your turn: who do you reckon he's been communicating with on Facebook?"

"His mum, of course," I said.

Hound smiled at me. "Exactly what I was thinking. So it's about time you paid Mrs. Bander your respects, don't you think?"

"Me?" I said, perhaps the smallest, most vulnerable "me" that had ever come from my mouth.

"She don't like me much," said Hound. "It's gotta be you."

HOME WITH THE ZOLTS

I remembered what Mrs. Jazy had said about there being "a vibrant community here in the seventies."

And I guess you could see vestiges of that. There was a mud-brick building, its middle collapsed like an unrisen cake, which looked like it might once have been a sort of community center. And next to this there was a playground, or what was left of a playground – the skeleton of a slide; a swing set without swings, a single rusty chain dangling.

There were no street signs anywhere, no street numbers, just a maze of tracks, so the only way to find Mrs. Bander's place was to ask. The first person I came across – a boy about my age but about five times my size – was sitting on an oil drum, spooning cocoa mix from the tin into his mouth.

"Hello," I said.

He eyed me suspiciously, before spooning some more cocoa.

"You couldn't tell me where Mrs. Bander's place is, could you?" I said.

"You're right, I couldn't," he said.

The second person was bent over the open hood of a car. He looked pretty wrecked – scrawly tatts, greasy hair, stained clothes. In contrast, his car – I think it was some sort of Monaro – was spotless, like something you'd see at one of those muscle car rallies.

"Excuse me," I said.

He looked up, a wrench in his hand.

"Why, you fart or something?" he said, laughing.

"Could you tell me where Mrs. Bander lives?" I asked.

"Depends," he said.

"Depends?"

He rubbed his thumb against his fingers.

Toby had ripped me off, the Hound had ripped me off, now this grease monkey wanted to rip me off as well.

No way, I told myself, as I kept on walking.

The third person I asked was a girl. She was around Toby's age and was sitting on an old car seat reading a book. At her feet was a dog even mangier than the others I'd seen, and behind her was an old school bus that was up on blocks.

"Hi," I said.

She looked up. Even though her long hair was in Heidi braids and the glasses she was wearing were lopsided, I could still see the family resemblance.

She must be the Zolt's younger sister, Zoe.

"Do you want to talk to my mother?" she said.

"If I could."

"She's probably still in bed."

I glanced at my watch: it was past eleven.

"She usually doesn't get up until midday," said Zoe Zolton-Bander.

My phone buzzed, so I took it out of my pocket. It was a message from Imogen: *where r u?*

"Is that the new model iPhone?" Zoe asked.

"Yes," I said.

She brought out an older model iPhone from her pocket.

"This is mine," she said. "It's truly pathetic."

"You want to check out mine," I said. "Got some sweet apps."

I showed her one I knew she'd like – the fake-a-call app.

"I wish that would work on my phone," she said.

"It will," I lied. "What's your number? I'll SMS it to you."

She hesitated, and I'm sure I could see a flicker of distrust on her face.

"Or I can Bluetooth it if you like," I said.

"SMS it," she said, before reciting her number.

I tapped the digits into my phone and stored them under *Zoe*.

Gotcha, I said to myself.

As I SMSed her the app I knew wouldn't work on her phone there was a hacking sound from inside the bus. Then the flush of a toilet.

"Mum's up," said Zoe.

A tough-sounding voice came from inside the bus. "Where's my coffee, Zoe?"

"Already in the microwave, Mum."

Silence, during which I imagined Mrs. Zolton-Bander finding her coffee, taking a gulp.

Then: "Who you talking to out there?"

"Dom," I mouthed.

"Dom," said Zoe.

"Dom who?"

"Silvagni," I mouthed.

"Silvagni," said Zoe.

"Any relation to the Bobby Silvagni the bookie?"

I shook my head.

"No," said Zoe.

"Good for him, then. Bloody prize rogue, Bobby."

I was feeling pretty pleased that I wasn't related to a bloody prize rouge like Bobby Silvagni when Mrs. Bander said, "Then who are you, Dom Silvagni?"

"I'm the president of your son's Facebook fan club," I called out.

"President of your son's Facebook fan club" was

Hound's idea. I didn't like it then, and I still didn't like it.

Mrs. Bander appeared, coffee cup in one hand, laptop in the other. I'd seen photos of her in the paper and online, so I thought I knew what to expect.

And she looked just like those photos: streaky blond hair parted down the middle, falling onto her shoulders; huge rectangular-framed sunglasses and puckered mouth. She was wearing a leopard-print top, black trousers and ornate earrings.

But she was wearing something else I wasn't expecting: a sort of presence, an authority, that immediately made me feel like a little kid.

She handed the laptop to her daughter and said, "Can you get my emails for me? Bloody computer's been playing up."

Zoe threw me the tiniest of smiles. I knew exactly what she was saying – old people, why are they so hopeless with technology?

Mrs. Bander turned her attention to me, staring at me for what seemed like ages, not even bothering to disguise the fact.

Eventually she said, "Well, you're certainly better-looking than that tub of lard Bobby Silvagni."

I wasn't sure how to respond to this, but then I remembered the mug I'd bought.

"This is for you," I said, handing it to her.

After removing the wrapping, fingernails flashing,

she turned the mug upside down.

"What does that say?" she said, handing the mug to her daughter. "Can't read without my glasses," she explained to me.

"*RBY Enterprises*," read Zoe.

"We're not getting a cut of this, are we?"

"No, we're not," said Zoe, handing the mug back to her mother.

"Thieving ratbags!" said Mrs. Bander.

And I have to admit, I rocked back a bit – I wouldn't want to be one of those thieving ratbags if she got her long, glossy nails on them.

"Can you show him them prices?" she said to Zoe.

Zoe tapped away at the keyboard and then showed me the screen. A Word document read:

Newspaper interview	*$500*
Newspaper interview (with photo)	*$650*
TV interview	*$2000*
Tour of Otto's bedroom	*$250*

"I wasn't really after an interview," I said.

"Then, darling, what are you doing here?" said Mrs. Bander, handing her daughter a pouch of tobacco.

"As you are probably aware, there are now almost a million and a half fans on your son's Facebook

fan page, and every one of them is hungry for new information about him," I said.

Zoe rolled a cigarette with nimble fingers and passed it to her mum. Mrs. Bander put it between her lips, lit it with a lighter, inhaled deeply, then blew two perfectly shaped plumes out of her nostrils.

"All the charges are there," she said, pointing at the laptop.

"I don't think you understand –" I started.

"Look, you think I came down in the last shower or something? All the numbers are there," she said.

"Okay, I understand," I said, holding up my hand. "I'm very sorry to have disturbed you."

"You know, I didn't think this app would work on my model," said Zoe, engrossed in her iPhone.

"Nice to have met you," I said. "I'll see you later."

What I really wanted to do was run as fast as I could out of here, past the greasy mechanic, past the cocoa-scoffing fat kid, all the way back to the main road.

But I didn't, I just walked quickly.

When I got back to the Hummer, Hound had all his hi-tech surveillance gear out.

"You stir the pot?" he asked.

"I think so," I said.

"Okay, let's see what happens."

As if on cue, a message flashed on the screen of his laptop: *Outgoing call to ... 0400 230592.*

"She's calling somebody on her mobile," said Hound.

"Hello, Sage," somebody answered.

"Look, I know you said we had to play a waiting game with these movie ..."

As the conversation progressed, Hound taking in every word, I zoned out.

He's tapping the wrong phone.

The Zolt wasn't communicating with his mother on Facebook. Because the Zolt's mother was computer illiterate – there was no way she had posted those Facebook entries. And, besides that, she just didn't seem like the sort of person who would be that concerned about her son's welfare.

No, he was communicating with somebody else.

Somebody who was computer literate. Who was much smarter. And kinder.

His sister.

That's whose phone he should have been tapping.

Still, I had to sit there for another hour while Hound listened to the wrong person having the wrong conversations.

Eventually, when the traffic to Mrs. Bander's phone stopped, Hound said he'd drop me off where I was staying.

STOLEN CAR

Just as Hound stopped outside the Jazys' front gate my phone beeped.

Text received from Zoe, it said.

I opened it, but there was nothing there.

That was weird, I thought, but I didn't think any further about it because Hound said, "I guess this is your stop, kid."

"Thanks," I said, but it was a reflex thanks, the kind my parents had taught me to say after somebody had done me a favor.

I went to open the car door when this ham of a hand slammed into the side of my head. It was so unexpected, so random, it took me a while to find any words.

"What did you do that for?"

"Just keep it real, okay, partner."

I stumbled out of the Hummer with my head

ringing, my ear stinging. Keyed the entry code in and went through the gates. Mr. Jazy was coming towards me, and he looked upset: angry face, angry facial hair.

"Where the blazes have you been, Dom?"

"I went for a run."

"You've been gone the whole morning."

"It was a long run."

"You realize that when you're staying with my family I'm responsible for you. I really can't have you taking off like that, without letting anybody know where you are."

"I'm sorry, Mr. Jazy," I said, and I really was sorry, he was really worked up. "It won't happen again."

"So you're okay?" he asked.

"Yes, I'm totally fine."

"Well, that's the main thing," said Mr. Jazy, putting his arm around my shoulder. "Come on, let's enjoy the afternoon's festivities."

There were cars parked on both sides of the drive, including Mr. Jazy's big classic Mercedes 450SEL 6.9, but one in particular was attracting a lot of attention. A group of men were standing around, stroking it, talking to it, lavishing it with car-love. Apparently, it was a Maserati Quattroporte. Apparently, it was worth two hundred and fifty thousand dollars.

I went inside, had a shower. As I was getting changed, Imogen's voice came from the other side of the door. "Dom, you in there?"

"Come in," I said, buttoning up my shirt.

Imogen came in and immediately I could tell that something was bothering her.

"This accident that Tristan had yesterday?" she said.

"That's right, the fall," I said, wondering how much she knew, if Tristan had told her something.

"You guys weren't doing drugs or anything, were you?" she said.

"No, of course not!" I said. "What's wrong?"

"It's just that Tristan seems a bit, I don't know, over the top."

"What's new?"

"No, seriously. There's something weird going on."

I was starting to feel a bit guilty about Tristan, a guilt I didn't get – he'd agreed to go to Gunbolt Bay, I hadn't forced him; and he'd pushed me off the boat, hadn't he?

I guess you can't argue with how you feel, though, and I felt guilty.

"I'll go and have a talk with him," I said.

The Jazys' charity barbecue was a pretty big deal. More cars were pulling up, and there were at least twenty boats hanging off the pier. A band was playing. There was face-painting for the little kids. A bouncy castle. Pony rides.

Tristan, wearing just board shorts, was standing

at the end of the jetty, looking out over the water.

It was a pretty weird pose, sort of heroic, the type of pose you'd adopt if you thought somebody was watching you.

But nobody was watching Tristan except for me, and he didn't know that.

"Hi, Tristan," I said. "How's it going?

"You know, I woke up this morning and I realized something: I almost got killed yesterday," he said, and there was something in his voice, like a mixture of joy and pride.

I was pretty sure they hadn't been shooting to kill, that if they had been we'd both be feeding the prawns right now. But I wasn't going to tell Tristan that.

"It was a pretty wild ride," I said, wondering why I wasn't feeling whatever it was he was feeling.

"You ever heard of Nietzsche?" said Tristan.

"Of course," I said, though the truth was I'd only heard the name, I didn't have a clue who he was.

"Nietzsche said that for exceptional people, the usual rules don't apply."

"Right," I said, because I couldn't think of anything else to say.

Imogen was right, there was something unhinged about Tristan.

He looked at me, smiled a blazing smile, and said, "Become what you are."

And then he hugged me. I'm not kidding, a great

big squeezy hug.

"That was the best day of my life," he said.

Further weird conversation was prevented by the buzzing arrival of not one but two helicopters. I hurried around to the other side of the house just in time to see them land within a few minutes of each other on the lawn. From the first one alighted Cameron Jamison, the man who'd given me a lift that morning. The second one contained my family: Dad, Mom, Miranda and Toby.

Now I knew why Mr. Jazy and his facial hair were freaking out so much. Imagine if my parents had arrived and I wasn't there, and the people who were looking after me had no idea where I was.

Big mummy hug from Mom. Big daddy hug from Dad.

Toby's nostrils were already twitching.

"Where's the food at?" he said.

But it was Miranda, my geek-genius sister, who I was really excited to see. "What's with the chopper?"

"Dad borrowed it from Rocco Taverniti," she said. Dropping her voice she added, "This thing looks even worse than I thought."

The Jazy parents and the Silvagni parents did their mutual admiration act and I had no difficulty getting Miranda away to the back of the house, out of sight of the rest of the partygoers.

"Imagine, he's probably out there somewhere,"

she said, standing exactly where Tristan had been, looking out over the rippled water.

"He's gone," I said.

"How can you be so sure?"

"You know, that sighting up north."

Miranda scoffed at that. "Yeah, right. That service station attendant has now come out and said it wasn't him he saw after all."

Where was Otto Zolton-Bander? Though I believed Hound's story I also had this feeling that the Zolt was still on the island.

I figured now was as good a time as any to bring up the subject, and I'd already thought of a clever way of doing it.

"How do you know if your phone's been tapped?" I asked.

"Why?"

"Because my phone's doing weird things, and I thought maybe it's being tapped," I lied.

Miranda raised one eyebrow, as if to say, *Why would anybody bother doing that?*

"It happened to a couple of kids at school," I said. Another lie.

"Okay, let's have a look," she said.

"There you go," I said, handing her my phone.

She inspected it, thumbs working overtime, before she said, "How do you feel about me jailbreaking this thing?"

"Do you have to?" I said, because I'd heard stories

at school about phones that had been jailbroken and then became bricked and didn't work anymore.

"Well, I need to go into the root files and that's the only way to do it."

As far as tech stuff went, I really trusted Miranda, but the doubt must've still been visible all over my little-brother face, because she said, "I'll be gentle."

Finally I relented. "Okay, jailbreak it, sis."

I always thought a jailbreak would be quite an event, lots of noise, lots of action, like a real jailbreak, but this was an anticlimax.

More thumb work, a couple of peeks at her own iPhone, a reboot, then Miranda said quietly, "There, it's done."

"But it looks the same," I said.

"It is the same," she said. "It's just that now we can have a look at the nuts and bolts."

After ten or so minutes of doing just that, she said, "There isn't a tap on your phone."

I felt a bit guilty sending her on a wild-goose chase like that; I knew there wasn't a tap on my phone and it hadn't taken me long to realize that I didn't have the necessary expertise to tap somebody else's phone.

"There's two," said Miranda.

At first I thought she was joking, but I know that geeks like her don't joke about geek stuff.

"You've got some spyware in your phone that's relaying all your calls, your texts, your data to a computer somewhere," she said.

"But how did it get there?"

"Did you open a text from somebody and there was nothing there?"

Zoe, the Zolt's sister!

"Yes," I said.

"That's when you inadvertently installed it," said Miranda. "Come to think of it, they could probably turn on your phone's microphone and listen in to this conversation we're having right now."

"They are?" I said.

"No, I said they could. The mike's off now. The other problem you've got is that the base station your phone is logged into isn't an authentic one. It's what we call an IMSI-catcher. They're also monitoring your calls. Probably even logging your position."

That had to be Hound, I thought, remembering all the hi-tech surveillance stuff he had in his Hummer.

"You are so owned," said Miranda.

I digested this information for a while before I said, "Okay, if they own me, can I own them without them knowing I own them?"

"What's going on, Dom?" Miranda said, an uncharacteristically serious note to her voice.

"Like I said, this kid at school's been tapping phones and –"

"In case, you hadn't noticed, I'm not a total idiot.

There's something going on, and it's not just this. Gus and Dad and you, you've got some sort of secret men's business happening."

More than anything I wanted to tell Miranda. Tell her about The Debt. About Gus's leg. About Dad. About everything. She was my sister, why shouldn't I? Unburden. Open my mouth and let it all come out.

"Let me guess – you can't tell me?" said Miranda.

I shook my head. "Not now I can't."

She was silent for a moment. "Okay, let's see what we can do about this phone of yours."

It took her a while, she even had to call a friend of hers for advice, but eventually she said, "Okay, this is how it works."

Just as she finished explaining it to me, I looked around and there was Imogen standing next to the bouncy castle.

I waved at her, but she didn't return my greeting.

I thanked Miranda and walked towards Imogen.

"What's happening?" I said, as I got closer.

"Have you seen –" she started, but the rest of her sentence was drowned out by the throaty roar of an accelerating sports car.

I scooted out to the front, Imogen just behind, in time to hear somebody yell, "It's the Maserati!" There was pandemonium, people running around everywhere.

"The Zolt," they kept saying.

The Zolt. The Zolt. The Zolt.

I moved towards the lawn where the helicopters had landed and there was Cameron Jamison, standing next to his sleek black chopper.

"You need some young eyes?" I yelled out to him.

"Sure," he said. "Get in."

I needed no further invitation. But as I ran over and jumped into the passenger's seat, I realized that Imogen was still behind me.

"I'm coming too," she said.

"Not a good idea," I said, thinking that she was not the person I wanted with me if I did actually come face-to-face with the Zolt.

She went to get in, and I really had no choice – I slid the Perspex door across. And by that time Cameron Jamison had started the engine and we were ready to take off.

As we ascended I looked down to see Imogen staring up at us, a hurt expression on her face, getting smaller and smaller until she disappeared from view.

"Don't the cops on the island have their own choppers?" I asked Cameron Jamison as we swept along the coast, following the main road.

Cameron laughed at that and said, "There's four cops on this island and they've got nothing, especially not a brain."

"That's a bit tough, isn't it?"

"Do you really think somebody with a brain would let a punk kid make them look like fools for such a long time?"

"There it is!"

Up ahead, the Maserati turned off the main road and onto a smaller road that led towards the interior of the island.

My phone rang. It was Mr. Jazy. "Is that you, Dom?"

"Yes."

"You're in the chopper, right?"

"Roger that," I said, for some reason adopting action-film language.

"So have you seen him?"

I thought of all the alpha males down below, in their Jaguars and their Porsches and their Mercedes, all dying to start playing catch the fugitive, waiting for some direction from the eye-in-the-sky, from me.

"Catch the Zolt," The Debt had told me. Not Mr. Jazy. Or Hound. Or the brainless cops. Me.

"Sorry, you're breaking up. I can't hear you. Reception's bad," I said before I hung up.

We were right on top of the Maserati as it accelerated up the road.

"He's really moving," said Cameron. "One eighty at least."

I imagined the Zolt below, all six foot five of him, working the gears.

"He's going way too fast," said Cameron.

I could see why he said this – up ahead was a T-junction.

Slow down, Zolt. Slow down.

But he didn't.

He overshot the junction, went into a slide, flipped over, rolled three times, then finally came to rest.

Cameron landed the chopper on the road, and I was out of the door almost before it had touched down.

I ran over to the crumpled Maserati.

Looked in through the open window. At the inflated air bag.

At Tristan!

He looked at me, smiled, and said, "Become what you are."

Then his eyes closed and he slumped forward, his face disappearing into the inflated air bag.

I ran back to the helicopter; where Cameron was holding his phone.

"It's not the Zolt," I said. "It's Tristan."

"His dad's on his way," said Cameron.

A few minutes later the first car arrived – a BMW. Then Mr. Jazy in his Mercedes. More and more cars. Then the police. An ambulance. Another ambulance.

I kept shrinking back, away from the Maserati, away from the crowd, away from Tristan.

But when I saw Imogen get out of the car that

Mrs. Jazy was driving I ran straight up to her.

"Thank goodness he's alive," I said, and I went to hug her.

But Imogen stepped away from me and my open arms.

"What happened yesterday?" she said, her arms folded across her chest. "What happened with you and Tristan?"

"Like I told you, we had this accident and –"

"Don't lie to me!" said Imogen.

I said nothing. What was there to say?

"Unless you tell me the truth, I'm never going to say another word to you as long as I live," said Imogen, her eyes locked on mine.

DEAD COLD HAND

I closed my eyes and they stayed closed; sleep was winning this particular battle.

"Darling, maybe we should head home now," said Mom, stroking my cheek with her forefinger.

She used to do this all the time when I was a little kid, but I couldn't remember the last time she'd done it. Suddenly I was back in that fuzzy world of childhood, cocooned in comfort and security.

It didn't last long, though, only as long as it took me to open my eyes and see where I was: in a waiting room in Mater Hospital.

Yes, Mater was the poshest hospital on the Gold Coast, more like a five-star hotel where the staff wore stethoscopes, and the waiting room had cable and an espresso machine and an array of gourmet chocolate cookies, but it was still a hospital.

I checked my watch: it was past one in the morning, and we'd been here since six the previous night, after Rocco Taverniti's helicopter had dropped us off at the hospital's helipad.

"You heard what Mr. Jazy said?" said Mom. "There's nothing we can do, now. We might as well head back to Halcyon Grove."

Yes, Mr. Jazy had said exactly that, about an hour ago. "Tristan is in a coma," he'd said. "But his condition is stable. We really appreciate your support, but you might as well head home now. We'll keep you informed as to his progress."

Everybody else had heeded Mr. Jazy's advice and gone home. Even Imogen.

"Come on, Dom. Let's go home," said Mom, a note of impatience in her voice.

"You can go," I said. "But I'm staying here."

"You're fifteen years old," said Mom. "I'm not leaving you here by yourself."

I planted my feet, folded my arms: *I'm staying.*

Mom was cross now; I could see it in her face.

But it didn't last long because she did that thing she often did: she went from cross Mom to problem-solver Mom.

Taking out her phone she said, "I'll be back in five minutes."

It actually took her ten minutes but when she returned she was smiling.

"Sorted," she said.

Not long afterwards our Cambodian cleaner, Hue Lin, walked in.

"I remembered that Hue Lin lives very close to here," said Mom, talking as if Hue Lin wasn't standing right next to her. "She's offered to look after you tonight."

After Mom had gone I looked sheepishly at Hue Lin. "Sorry," I said.

"Nothing to be sorry about," she said. "Your mother is paying me double dollars."

She took an enormous book out of her bag – *Preparative Chromatography of Fine Chemicals and Pharmaceutical Agents* – opened it to a bookmarked page and started reading.

I watched television, flicking through the channels, nothing capturing my interest for more than a few minutes.

Then I fell asleep for a while.

When I woke I thought: *Cookies!*

I started at the Hedgehogs, moved on to the Mint Slices.

By the time I reached the Tim Tams I was feeling pretty bloody yucky.

That way-too-much-sugar-for-breakfast sort of pretty bloody yucky.

So I left the waiting room to go to the bathroom, maybe even see if I could have a shower, and Mrs.

Jazy walked right past me.

"Mrs. Jazy!" I said.

She turned around and looked at me, and I could tell that she was struggling to put me into context.

Eventually she said, "Dominic, what are you still doing here?"

I shrugged.

I wondered how much she knew. Had Tristan told her something about the trip in the speedboat? Had she guessed, the way mothers do, that something had happened?

"You really don't need to hang around," she said.

Again, a shrug.

"If you saw Tristan, then would you go home?" she said.

I nodded.

"Okay," she said. "This way."

I walked with her down the corridor, stopping at a room that said *Intensive Care 2B*.

I followed Mrs. Jazy inside.

Tristan was on the bed. White face on white pillowcase. Eyes closed. Motionless.

On the outside, nothing was happening. However, the array of buzzing, beeping, blinking monitors indicated that on the inside things were still going. Lungs were inflating and deflating. His heart was pumping. Blood was circulating. Inside, he was alive. But outside, nothing happened.

Mr. Jazy was sitting by his son's side, in an orange chair.

He said nothing to me, just indicated another orange chair on the other side of the bed. *Sit down*.

I did just that.

"I'm sorry, Tristan," I whispered. "I'm really sorry."

A series of images flashed through my mind: inviting myself to his summer house, setting it up for us to go look for the Zolt, the trip in the speedboat, getting shot at, the escape, following in the chopper as the Maserati overshot the T-junction.

I put my hand over Tristan's hand. It felt so cold, so dead.

Again that series of flashbacks. It occurred to me that my memory was trying to tell me something, but what was it?

Tristan's monitors kept buzzing, beeping, blinking.

The door pushed open and a nurse entered.

Her eyes took me in and she said, her accent Irish, "I'm sorry, but we really can't be allowing any visitors now."

"That's okay," I said, getting up.

Mrs. Jazy smiled at me.

"You'll go home now, won't you, Dominic?"

I nodded.

Mr. Jazy rummaged in his beard and then held out his hand for me to shake it.

Again, I wondered how much they knew.

I took his hand; his grip was surprisingly strong, and I flinched a bit.

Back in the waiting room, Hue Lin was still reading her book.

"I'm going home now," I told her.

We both went downstairs and she watched as I got into a taxi.

"Where we going?" the driver asked.

"Gold Coast," I said. "Halcyon Grove."

We were on the freeway and the sun was coming up on our left, spinning out of the sea.

Again, I dozed off.

I woke to the sound of my phone beeping.

Mom, I thought. Checking up on me.

Or maybe news of Tristan.

But it wasn't.

It was a text from Zoe Zolton-Bander.

need to talk urgent on bus meet me central bus station 8am

"So Halcyon Grove's past the Robina turnoff, right?" the driver asked.

"Change of destination," I said. "We're going to Central Bus Station, instead."

"The Chinese lady at the hospital said to take you

to Halcyon Grove," said the driver.

I pulled out the money Mom had given me and waved it at him.

"The Chinese lady at the hospital is actually Cambodian," I said. "And she isn't paying the fare, I am."

"Fair enough," said the driver as he swung the wheel and headed for the next exit.

TURTLE TIME

I walked into the cafeteria at Central Bus Station and Zoe was sitting in one corner.

Standing back, I watched her for a while, concerned that this was some sort of setup, that she had an accomplice.

Because really, how far could I trust her? She'd put a whole lot of spyware on my phone. Her brother was a notorious criminal. And her mother was … well, I'm not too sure what her mother was, but I knew she definitely wasn't to be trusted either.

The accomplice could be her, I thought, clocking the backpacker sitting at the next table. Or him, the businessman on his phone. Or even one of them, that gaggle of Japanese tourists.

But then I realized how paranoid I was becoming. Eventually, inevitably, you have to trust somebody. Sort of.

"Hi," I said, approaching her table.

Immediately she got up, whispering, "Let's get out of here."

"Why?"

"We're being watched." She nodded her head to indicate the person at the adjacent table.

He looked pretty anonymous: a lumpy, bald middle-aged man engrossed in the sports pages of the paper. Zoe, however, was very keen to get away from him.

"What was that all about?" I asked after we'd left the café.

"We have to be careful," said Zoe, adjusting her glasses.

"Then where do you want to go?" I said.

"Just somewhere very public."

"How about the zoo? It's only about ten minutes' walk."

"Perfect," said Zoe Zolton-Bander. "Purr-fect."

It was school vacation, so there was a long line of people waiting to get in.

"I don't do lines," Zoe said, and the next time a family went through she just tacked on to the end of it.

I followed her lead.

I hadn't been to the zoo for years, not since I was a little kid. It'd changed a lot since then, all the

concrete and bars had been replaced by enclosures, designer cages.

It still sounded the same, all those animal sounds – the bellows, trumpets, squawks and chatterings – and it smelled the same too, like poo, zoo poo.

"Anywhere in particular?" I said.

"I don't like monkeys that much," said Zoe.

"Overrated?"

"Totally, especially those ones with the Technicolor bums."

We avoided the monkeys, especially those with the Technicolor bums, and found a seat in front of the Galápagos turtle enclosure.

There weren't any people here and the two turtles seemed to like it like that, not doing anything much to attract a crowd.

"Okay, me first," I said. "How did you know I was back in the Gold Coast?"

"Reverie isn't a big place," she said.

"So you caught an overnight bus just to see me?"

Zoe nodded. "My turn now." She scanned the area before she said, "You're a liar. You are so not the president of my brother's fan club."

"So what? You tapped my phone," I said.

"You were so going to tap mine," she said. "I just got in first."

When an elderly couple approached, Zoe tensed.

"Relax," I said.

They shuffled in front of us, peering out into the enclosure.

"What in the blazes is this supposed to be?" asked the man.

"It's the Galápagos turtles, sir," I said.

"They doing anything?" asked the woman.

"No, not a lot. Just eating some vegetables."

"Ludicrous," said the man, then the two of them wandered off.

Zoe waited until they were well out of sight before she said in a level voice, "Do you want to start again?"

"I think that's a good idea," I said. "Why did you contact me?"

Zoe considered my question, in much the same way as one of the Galapágos turtles was now considering the piece of cabbage in front of its nose.

She sighed, as if she had just made a momentous decision. "Because I thought you might know where Otto is."

"You don't?" I said, not bothering to disguise the surprise in my voice.

"Not anymore."

"Not since he got away from Hound de Villiers?"

"Hound de Villiers is a moron."

"I don't know – he did figure out where your brother was."

"Only because somebody told him."

"Somebody?" I said, but I already had a fair idea of who that somebody was.

"Your mum?" I said.

Zoe nodded. "Otto didn't get away, he was taken away."

"How do you know that?" I asked, remembering Hound's story about the boat with the ASIO types aboard.

"Because if Otto had gotten away by himself, he would've contacted me."

"Using your Facebook code – sorry, concealment."

There was surprise on Zoe's face as she said, "You know about that?"

"Let's see," I said, trying to think of a concealment for "yes." "Yacht side smell."

Zoe smiled. "He would've used Facebook, he would've gotten in touch somehow."

"Instead of stealing a plane and flying it over the city?"

"You really think my brother would pull a cheap stunt like that?" Zoe said.

"I was there."

"So you saw him with your very own eyes, did you, even though he was hundreds of meters away?"

The turtle, having decided that the cabbage was not to its liking, had moved on to a piece of cauliflower. And I needed to take a breather; too much information too quickly and my brain was having difficulty processing it.

Eventually I said, "So what are you saying, that your brother's been kidnapped?"

"That's exactly what I'm saying."

"But by who?"

Absent all day, the sun had appeared in a chink in the clouds. Suddenly it was warm. Zoe took off her hat, shook out her hair.

"Why do you want to catch my brother so much?" she asked.

The obvious answer, the logical answer, was, "The reward, of course," but something told me this wasn't going to cut it with Zoe. She was clever, she would've done a background check on me, found that my father was one of the richest men in Queensland.

"Not for the reward, if that's what you're thinking," I said. "I don't need the money. It's the challenge. The cops couldn't bring him in. Hound ended up with empty handcuffs. I thought I could be the kid who caught the Zolt."

Again Zoe took time, turtle time, to consider what I'd just said.

She must've found my answer satisfactory, because she said, "I really don't know why somebody would want to kidnap my brother."

"Maybe it's something he knows," I said.

She considered this for a while.

"I've just got this funny idea that the safest place for my brother right now is actually in jail."

She was right: it was a funny idea, but I didn't have time to think just how funny it was, because two men in jeans and leather jackets appeared near the meerkat enclosure and started walking towards us.

"Cops!" said Zoe, getting up quickly, ready to make a run for it.

It was too late, however; they were almost on us.

"Federal Government," the taller of the two said, bringing out a wallet, flashing some sort of badge.

Wow, I thought. Zoe had a right to be so paranoid.

"You're Dominic Silvagni?" he said.

"That's me," I said, wondering how he knew my name.

"We'd like you to accompany us to answer a few enquiries we have."

"I think you've got the wrong person," I said, looking at Zoe, sister and accomplice of the notorious criminal Otto Zolton-Bander.

"Dominic Silvagni?" said the shorter man. "Resident of Halcyon Grove? Born seventeenth of February, 1997?"

"Yes, that's me."

"Then you're the right person, alright. Let's go, buddy."

"You're a minor!" said Zoe. "They're not allowed to question you without a guardian being present."

I'm sure Zoe was right, but I also figured that I might as well get this – whatever it was – over with.

"It's okay," I said to her. "Let's stay in touch."

We left, leaving Zoe alone with the Galápagos turtles. The two men said nothing as I got into the backseat of a dark car that was parked right outside the zoo in a No Parking zone.

"Where are you taking me?" I asked.

"You'll find out," said the taller man.

Ten minutes later we pulled into the parking lot of an anonymous-looking office building and they told me to get out. I followed them through a back door, down anonymous-looking corridors and into an anonymous-looking room.

I sat down. They sat down.

They looked at me. I looked at them.

Who were they?

"Could I possibly have a look at your badge, again?" I said.

The taller cop reached into his pocket, brought out a wallet, and flicked it open in front of my face.

The badge certainly looked like the real thing: there was a kangaroo and an emu and the words "Australian Federal Police."

"Okay," I said.

Even if it wasn't the real thing, even if they were impersonating Federal cops, I was intrigued as to what they wanted from me.

"Dominic, we'd like to talk to you about Otto Zolton-Bander," said the shorter cop.

"Sure," I said, because I figured there was no use denying that I didn't know of him.

"From what we understand, you and Mr. Jazy may have visited his hideaway recently."

"We may have," I said, but already I had this feeling that I was getting out of my depth here.

"So what we need you to do is tell us everything that happened yesterday," said the shorter cop.

"Take your time," said the other cop.

Getting further and further out of my depth.

But I did as they asked and I was back at Reverie Island.

I was in the helicopter with Cameron Jamison. And I was looking in through the open window. At the inflated air bag. Tristan saying, "Become what you are." I was running back to the helicopter. Where Cameron was holding his mobile phone.

"It's not the Zolt," I was saying. "It's Tristan."

"His dad's on his way," Cameron Jamison said.

But how did Cameron Jamison know that it was Tristan in the car? Why hadn't he assumed it was the Zolt like everybody else?

Really, there was only one answer to that question: Cameron knew it wasn't the Zolt because he had the Zolt!

"Dominic?" said the shorter cop. "What can you tell us?"

I remembered what Zoe had said: "They're not allowed to question you without a guardian being present."

"I want a guardian present!" I said.

But as soon as I said that, I realized that my mum or my dad were the last people I wanted here.

"Actually, I want my lawyer," I said.

The two men exchanged looks.

"Let's keep the lawyers out of this, shall we?" said the shorter one.

"I want my lawyer," I said.

The other cop shrugged. "You're making a dumb move, but you do have a right to call your lawyer."

Problem was, I didn't have a lawyer.

I scrolled through my iPhone looking for somebody who at least vaguely resembled a member of the legal profession. Jeremy Gallard's mother was this hotshot barrister, but Jeremy had been caught twice stealing from the school canteen, so they sort of canceled each other out. Really there wasn't anybody, but I certainly didn't want the cops to know that.

They were clever, they knew every cop trick in the cop book, and I needed all the help I could get.

So I called Gus. As I did the shorter man got up and left the room.

"Dom?" answered Gus.

"Mr. Giuseppe," I said. "It's Dominic Silvagni here."

"Dom," said Gus "What's going on?"

"That's right, Mr. Giuseppe –" I started, but then the line dropped out.

I was about to dial again but the taller cop said, "You can go if you like, Dominic."

"I can go?"

"You can go."

The other cop came back into the room and I noticed that he gave his partner a sort of wink.

"We'll drop you back at the zoo, if you like," he said.

"Can you take me home?" I said.

"Sure."

Outside the wind had picked up, and black clouds were banking up towards the ocean. The cops dropped me off outside the gates of Halcyon Grove, but as I made for my house, my phone beeped.

It was a message from Zoe: *you ok?*

But as I went to reply there was another beep, different from the last one.

There was a message on the screen that said: *Warning! Unauthorized Base Station is attempting to connect to your phone. Accept or Reject?*

It took me a while to realize that it was the app Miranda had installed, the anti-tapping app.

And I remembered how one cop had left the room while I was making the call to Gus.

The cops were trying to tap my phone!

How dare they?

I was just about to choose "Reject" when I had second thoughts: maybe I should play along with them, maybe I should let them listen to my calls for a while, and hopefully they'd soon realize that I wasn't some criminal mastermind and leave me alone.

I knew it was risky, but I chose "Accept."

Back in my bedroom, I opened Facebook on my laptop and went to the Zolt fan page.

I created a phony Facebook profile, calling myself the Technicolor Monkey, and even found a photo of one for my profile picture.

And I added an entry.

Zolt no expert

Straightaway I got a couple of replies – *yes he is!* and *your an idiot* – but neither was from Hera so I ignored them. I waited for another half an hour but there were no further replies, so I went to bed to get some much-needed sleep.

When I woke up, I discovered that Hera had replied to my post.

You are stupid!

I entered my own reply.

Idiot!

kids can own show

we smash ordinary

heros via sms

or fight to oblivion

Okay, it probably wasn't going to win the school poetry prize, but it worked, because it only took a minute for her to reply.

legs have ten toes

men have even feet

Ω Ω Ω

Gus was sitting outside his house, reading a book.

"I'm running in the Reverie Island All-Comers Mile Race on Saturday," I told him. "And you're driving me there."

Of course, he had a thousand reasons – most of them pretty good – why this was a bad idea.

"Okay, then," I said. "You're not driving me."

"That's the ticket," he said.

"I'll hitchhike instead, and just hope I'm not picked up by some homicidal maniac."

Silence, then a sigh, and then Gus saying, "We'll leave at six Saturday morning."

"That's the ticket," I said.

A RACE WORTH WINNING?

For somebody whose whole life has been about speed, about getting runners to run as fast as they can, Gus is a very slow driver. Yes, his old truck is a very slow truck, but he drives his very slow truck very slowly. Even the music he plays – delta blues – is slow music.

The only conversation we had as we slowly made our way very slowly to Reverie Island was racing conversation, Gus warning me how ruthless these professionals could be. Telling me stories to illustrate their ruthlessness.

When eventually we got to the island, there was an hour before the race was due to start. Many of the roads, including the main street, had been closed to traffic, and there was multicolored bunting strung everywhere; the race was obviously a big deal. And as we registered I could feel those characteristic

butterflies in my stomach. I was racing today! I quickly came to my senses, however. Racing wasn't why I was here. I told Gus that I'd see him at the starting line before the start time.

"That's fine," he said and I figured he knew that this trip was more about The Debt than running some crazy race.

There were only a few people in the café: a couple deep in conversation, their noses almost touching, and a hippie-looking character with a tangle of hair in her face and scruffy clothes.

I ordered a Zoltocino, sat down in a corner, and waited.

I was pretty worried: already she was five minutes late, and our plan depended on meticulous timing. After fifteen minutes of waiting I knew I should never have trusted her.

And to make matters worse the hippie was making for my table. Was she looking for a hand-out? Did she want to sell me drugs? Who knows, but I was pushing my chair back, ready to escape, when the hippie mouthed, "Dom."

I was thinking, *How does that hippie know my name?* when I realized that the hippie wasn't a hippie at all.

"Got you," said Zoe Zolton-Bander.

"Whatever," I said.

She sat down at the table and I said, "You get them?"

Her hand went into her pocket and when it reappeared it was holding five SIM cards, each from a different carrier.

"And they're all ..." I began to say, before I bit my tongue – of course they were all okay; this was a Zolton-Bander I was dealing with, not some amateur.

"Okay, let's get to work," she said.

"Here?"

"It's as safe as anywhere."

We got to work.

We spent half an hour swapping SIM cards in and out of phones, sending texts to my number. When we'd finished I put my SIM card back into my phone and turned it on.

"So you're sure they're monitoring your texts?" she said.

I opened Miranda's app. *Warning! Unauthorized base station is connected to your phone.*

"Definitely," I said.

I composed a text: *first meeting of teenage hacker society today at 4 @ 242 the esplanade, reverie island.* And sent it to the other five phone numbers. By now I only had fifteen minutes until starting time.

After going through the plan once more with Zoe, I left my backpack with her, and hurried back through town. The race really was a big deal; there were people everywhere, lining the route. I'd considered not going through with the race, but

I'd eventually decided that wasn't a good idea. The race was my reason for coming to the island, and as much as I didn't feel like running, I needed to make sure I didn't blow my cover.

Back at the starting line the other runners were already out of their tracksuits, already warming up.

Gus was standing there with a worried look on his face, which disappeared when he saw me approaching.

"Just treat it as a training run," he said. "You're not out to win anything."

"I'm not?"

"Look, I know what these charity runs are like. These rich types put up a grand just to make it a bit interesting. That may not be much to them, but it's a fair bit to some poor fellow on the pro circuit. Don't even try to mix it with them, Dom. They're as mean as junkyard dogs."

Just as he finished telling me this, an announcement came over the loudspeaker.

"Ladies and gentlemen, some exciting news! Local supporter Mr. Cameron Jamison has matched the previous prize money, so our runners today will now be competing for two thousand dollars."

I could see Cameron Jamison himself, standing at the back of the crowd. Our eyes met and a wry smile appeared on his face. Immediately, I looked away.

"Junkyard dogs," repeated Gus.

As I stood on the starting line, I could see exactly what Gus meant: quite a few of the other runners had the half-starved look of the semiprofessional athlete. They looked around, their cold eyes sizing up the competition.

"On your marks! Get ready! Go!" said the starter, and there was a huge cheer as we took off down the main street.

Already there was pushing and shoving, elbows flying everywhere. So I immediately removed myself from the traffic, running out wide, close to where the spectators were.

Just a leisurely two-kay stroll, I told myself as we left the town. Taking in the wonderful postcard-worthy scenery.

But around the half-kay mark, when a bunch of five runners suddenly increased the pace, I couldn't help myself: I went with them. Even with Gus's "treat it as a training run" looping through my head, I went with them.

One of the junkyard dogs looked behind, saliva dripping from his canines, and told me that my company wasn't appreciated, though not exactly in those words.

I dropped off the pace.

Another runner came up alongside me. He was tall, sinewy, fresh-faced; nothing doglike about him at all.

"Do you know how much longer it is?" he asked.

"Four or five hundred, I reckon."

"Thanks," he said before he kicked, moving rapidly away from me.

He had a nice uncomplicated style and looked a likely winner to my eyes. But when he caught up with the leading pack, and went to move past, one of the junkyard dogs put his paw out and tripped him up. He hit the ground hard, rolling a couple of times, ending up sprawled on his stomach.

"You okay?" I said, stopping next to him.

"I'm okay," he said. "You go get 'em, buddy, go get those mongrels."

I looked up: the mongrels were a fair way ahead now.

You're only on a training run, said one part of me as I took off. *This is just an alibi*, said another. But yet another part was having none of this.

I shifted up a gear, quickly making ground on the leaders. Luckily for me none of them had kicked yet; they were still in a tight knot, jostling for position. And when I say *jostling*, that's exactly what I mean – this looked more like mobile wrestling than running.

When we turned back into the main street, I was right behind them. And when the finish line banner came into sight, about a hundred meters away, they all kicked at the same time.

I was ready for that, though, and went with them, running out wide.

With fifty meters to go there were three of us left, then there were two: me and the man who'd had impolite words with me earlier.

With twenty meters to go, I could see the pain contorting his face, I could hear the raggedness of his breath.

I felt good, I felt great.

I thought of what Gus said about two grand not being much to a rich person, but being a quite a bit to some poor runner on the pro circuit. I slowed down and let the junkyard dog and his ragged breathing catch up. But when the finish line was within reach, a surge of energy, of power, of pride, of something, picked me up and took me over the line first.

The junkyard dog came over to congratulate me.

"Well done," he said, before his voice dropped. "You're dead, kid."

"I don't want the money," I said. "You can have it."

"Don't insult me," he said.

Gus was equally as unimpressed.

"Didn't you listen to what I said?"

"Hey, I won the race, didn't I?"

"This wasn't a race worth winning."

I checked my watch.

"I have to go," I told Gus.

"You do what you've got to do," he said. The light was falling on his face, on all the cracks and

crevasses, in such a way that it resembled some outback landscape. “You want me to wait for you?”

I did want him to wait – it was such a comforting thought – but it seemed to be almost an invitation to failure; I had to catch the Zolt and I had to do it by myself.

“No, it’s okay,” I said, “I’ll find my own way to the Gold Coast.”

Gus opened his mouth, and I could guess what he was about to say – *I can’t just leave you here* – but a look of resignation appeared on his face, and his mouth closed again.

I was about to take off when something occurred to me.

“Can you pick up my prize money for me?”

He gave me a dirty look but, hey, he didn’t owe his Mafioso brother three hundred bucks, not to mention the vig, did he?

PULL THE PLUG ON IT

I met Zoe at the prearranged meeting point, just outside the shop where Imogen had bought the postcards that day.

As she handed me my backpack, a car pulled up, all gleaming paint and mirror-polish chrome.

I knew the driver – he was the tattooed man with the long greasy hair I'd met a few days ago. The one who'd wanted me to pay him for pointing out where Zoe's place was.

"Are you sure we can trust him?" I asked Zoe before I got in.

"He's my Uncle Doug," said Zoe, giving me a scathing look.

That seemed even more reason not to trust him, but we didn't have a lot of time so I got into the car.

"Just don't make a mess back there," said Uncle Doug before he took off.

If Gus was incapable of driving fast, Uncle Doug was incapable of driving slow. Even when we were going slow, he was driving fast, double-clutching, hammering through the gears.

When we pulled up near the Jazy house he said, "Youse better not have made a mess back there," and took off.

"What did you tell him we were doing?" I asked Zoe.

"I told him nothing."

"But didn't he want to know?"

"We're not that sort of want-to-know family," she said.

I punched the code into the keypad of the Jazys' property, the gates clicked open and we slipped inside.

The key to the speedboat was in the same hiding place.

The engine started first turn.

Zoe undid the rope.

I put it into reverse and pressed down on the accelerator.

The boat surged forward, crashing into the pier.

"What are you doing?" Zoe asked as she picked herself up from the floor. "You told me you knew how to drive a boat!"

"I do," I said, making sure that this time it really was in reverse.

I pressed tentatively on the accelerator.

The boat moved backwards.

When we were clear of the pier, I put it into first and pointed the bow in the direction of Cameron Jamison's house.

When Tristan was behind the wheel, driving the boat had seemed like the easiest sort of driving you could do. There were no traffic signs to obey, no other traffic to worry about, just one big wide watery road. But now that it was me behind the wheel I could see that it was much trickier than it looked. For a start, there was all that power, those two bulbous outboards on the back. Even if I pressed my foot down a little bit, the boat seemed to respond a lot. And today it wasn't dead calm like it was the other day. There was quite a lot of wind, the bay was a flurry of waves, and the boat bounced around erratically, occasionally sending a fine spray up over us.

As we rounded a headland and the rear of Cameron Jamison's villa came into view, I slowed down. Zoe delved into her bag, pulled out a pair of binoculars and trained them on the shore.

I smiled at her; as far as accomplices went, she was turning out to be a pretty good one.

"There's only one speedboat there," she said, passing me the binoculars.

She was right: there was only one speedboat. A twin outboard like the one we had borrowed.

I could see no signs of movement.

I motored a bit closer to the headland, out of view of the villa, before I tossed the anchor over.

"You're going to swim from here?" Zoe asked, surprised.

"If we get any closer it'll look too suspicious," I said, peeling off my T-shirt.

I checked the contents of the backpack – a pair of pliers, a rubber plug with a cord attached – before I put it on my back, tightening the straps.

Then I slid over the side of the boat and into the water.

Ω Ω Ω

Twenty minutes later when I hoisted myself on board again, the wind had dropped to nothing and the sea was glassy. The shore was so still, it seemed painted, like a backdrop at the theatre. And this stillness seemed enormous, insurmountable, as if nothing could shift it.

"Any problems?" Zoe asked.

"No, I did it."

Zoe checked her phone.

"Two minutes to go," she said.

I checked my watch.

"I've got three," I said.

"Two, three, whatever – something should be happening by now!"

There were so many variables in our plan, so many things that could go wrong; I couldn't blame

Zoe for being worried.

Fifteen minutes later and she wasn't worried any longer, because basically she'd given up.

"You got wet for nothing, buddy," she said. "Let's get out of here."

"Just give it a few more minutes," I said, starting the motor, maneuvering the boat closer to the villa. "Remember, my text said that the meeting was at four. Surely they're going to allow for latecomers."

Zoe rolled her eyes and went to say something, but I cut her off.

"Be quiet!"

"Why?"

"Just be quiet."

Zoe did as I asked.

"Hear that?" I whispered.

The sound of cars, of people yelling, of wood splintering.

Zoe brought the binoculars back up to her eyes.

"Ohmigod," she said. "Ohmigod!" One of those I-can't-believe-my-eyes kind of ohmigods.

"What?"

But I already knew what.

I could see three figures, one barefoot, much taller than the other two, coming through the back door, heading down to the pier, getting onto the speedboat. My plan had worked: the cops had flushed them out.

"Is it your brother?"

She nodded.

"Looks like they've got a gun on him," I said.

"I know them," said Zoe. "The Mattner brothers."

"Mean?"

"Put it this way, when they were at school they used to bite the heads off live snakes."

"Okay, that's reasonably mean."

The speedboat started up and headed out to sea. "How long do you reckon it's going to take?" asked Zoe.

"According to my research, about five minutes," I said.

I kept my distance – I didn't want them using us as target practice.

"Were those Mattner boys into lighting fires as well?" I asked.

"How did you know that?"

"Technically, then, they're psychopaths," I said.

Meaning that they lacked empathy, would feel no remorse if they were forced to dispose of a couple of troublesome teenagers.

"The boat's pretty low in the water," said Zoe.

I took the binoculars.

Zoe was right, the boat was sinking, and sinking rapidly.

I'd replaced the drainage plug at the rear of the boat with a rubber plug, and then tied it off on the pier. As soon as they'd moved off, they'd pulled the plug out. The boat had been taking in water ever since.

"Shouldn't we get a bit closer to them?" Zoe asked.

"Not while they can still take a shot at us," I said. "You can't be too careful with psychopaths."

But almost before I said this the boat disappeared under the surface and its three occupants were sent sprawling into the water.

There was no way they could take a shot at us now, so I started the motor and made towards them.

When we got closer I could see that both Mattners had grabbed life jackets while Otto was managing without.

"Otto!" yelled Zoe.

"Zoe, is that you?"

I'd never heard Otto Zolton-Bander speak before. But given that he was six foot five, given that he was the Zolt, a notorious criminal, I'd expected a deep manly voice, the sort of voice that terrorizes citizens and steals planes. But he had a high-pitched voice, a squeaky voice, the sort of voice that belonged to one of the minor characters in a Disney cartoon.

"You okay?" Zoe called out.

"I'm okay," squeaked Otto.

"Okay," said Zoe.

Enough with the okays, already.

"Otto, we're going to pick you up," I yelled. "But I don't want them anywhere near my boat."

Otto was quick on the uptake, I'll give him that. Quick on the uptake, and equally quick on the duck-dive, because suddenly he was no longer there.

"He's definitely a good swimmer, right?" I asked Zoe.

"You watch," she said.

I watched and I watched and I watched.

Only an elite diver could hold their breath for this long, I thought.

But then he surfaced right next to the boat and we pulled him on board. And it was such a weird feeling: somebody who had only existed on the net, on a poster taped to a lamppost, on Fox News, was here, live in 3-D.

The Zolton-Banders embraced and I felt a tinge of jealousy: my younger sibling was more about vigs than hugs. Zoe looked towards me and mouthed "thank you."

I turned the boat around so that it was headed back to the shore.

"You can't leave us here!" yelled one of the Mattners.

"Save us!" yelled the other.

For one small second I thought about picking them up.

But then I realized what a mistake it would be to let them and their lack of empathy and inability to feel remorse in the boat.

Yes, they were obviously poor swimmers, but they did have life jackets and the water was warm.

I pressed on the accelerator and both Otto and Zoe gave the Mattners a one-fingered wave as we passed them.

As I steered the boat towards the Jazys' house, Zoe and Otto sat in the stern and talked. The wind whipped most of their words away, but I heard enough to know that Otto wasn't totally convinced that he should turn himself in to the police.

"But the Mattners will kill you," said Zoe.

Otto said something in reply, but I only caught the last few words: "... leave a pretty corpse."

Zoe wrapped her arms around her sodden brother. And she started crying. By the time we pulled into the pier he appeared to have given in to his kid sister.

"Otto's agreed that we can take him in," said Zoe. "Just as long as it's not to the local cops."

He looked at me for a while and I had this feeling that he was weighing me up. Then, in that incongruously high-pitched voice of his, he said, "If I turn myself in, what say you and me split the reward money?"

"Split it?" I said, because to be honest I'd forgotten all about the reward money.

"Yeah, fifty-fifty. Seeing as I'm making it so easy for you and all."

So easy?

I thought of Tristan in the hospital bed, his hand so cold and dead. The wordless Imogen.

"That's not going to happen," I said.

Again Otto studied my face.

He knew I didn't have a gun.

He knew that he could just walk away and there was nothing I could do to stop him.

"It's your sister who deserves that money, not you," I said.

Otto looked at me, then at his sister.

"You trust this guy?" he asked Zoe.

"I don't trust anybody," she said. "But do I think he'll share the money? Sure."

"Okay, so how we going to do this?"

I told him.

When I'd finished he said, "The Zolt is nobody's passenger."

Which is why we ended up in the Jazys' garage, removing the cover from Mr. Jazy's beloved Mercedes.

"I'll go and find the keys," I said.

"Don't bother," said the Zolt, feeling under the dash and yanking out two wires.

He put one of the wires in his mouth and stripped the insulation with his teeth. Repeated the process with the other wire. Joined the two wires together and the engine started.

"Let's blow this joint," he said in his squeaky voice, getting behind the wheel and revving the engine.

I got into the front seat, Zoe got in the back.

He backed the car expertly out of the garage. I got out of the car, punched the code in, and got back into the car as the gates slid open. To reveal a car parked across the driveway. Hound de Villiers's Hummer. Hound de Villiers was standing in front of it. He had a smile. And a gun. And it was pointed directly at the Zolt's head.

If I had a gun pointed between my eyes, I'm not sure how I'd react. Pee my pants? Probably. Put up my hands to surrender? Definitely. I so wouldn't do what the Zolt did, which was let out a banshee scream, jam his foot on the accelerator and head straight for Hound.

Hound de Villiers brought the gun up, took careful aim and squeezed the trigger.

Zoe screamed. I screamed, bringing up my forearms to protect my face. And the windshield fragmented.

I looked over at the Zolt and he was dead.

Well, that's what I expected, but he wasn't dead at all.

He was still conscious, still driving, still emitting that banshee scream.

Again, Hound took aim, but our car was almost on him and he had no time to squeeze the trigger.

He jumped out of the way just in time, and we rammed his Hummer. Metal crunched and our momentum pushed it forward about a meter.

Otto reversed the big car and charged again, this time aiming for the back end of the Hummer. It worked: when we hit the Hummer it spun around like a turnstile and we were through onto the road.

A bullet whistled past.

Zoe screamed. I screamed.

I looked behind.

Hound de Villiers put down his gun, got back into his Hummer.

It started to move forward, but then stopped. Smoke was coming from under the hood.

"That's the end of Hound," I said.

"I didn't think he would actually shoot me!" said the Zolt, flicking fragments of glass from his cheeks.

He sounded quite shocked.

"He really doesn't like you very much," I said as we tooled up the road.

There was the sound of a police siren and then a police car, lights flashing, flew past in the opposite direction.

"I don't think we're going to get off the island," I said.

The Zolt smiled.

"Not by car, we're not," he said.

THE STANDOFF

As we bounced over the back roads, Otto Zolton-Bander talked. About how Cameron Jamison had kept him captive. About how Cameron Jamison had said he was going to let him go once he had a movie deal stitched up. Once he had the book rights sorted.

It was a pretty amazing story, but something about it didn't quite ring true to me.

"So that was it?" I said. "That's all he wanted from you?"

"That's it," said the Zolt.

"And he didn't hurt you or anything?" I said.

"Uncle Cam, hurt me?" he said.

"Uncle Cam?" I said.

"He's not really my uncle," said the Zolt.

This whole thing was getting crazier and crazier.

"He is my godfather, but," said the Zolt.

"Our dad and Cameron Jamison were once business partners," explained Zoe.

"And then our dad got dead and Uncle Cam got rich," said her brother.

Too much information too quickly – I was getting indigestion of the brain.

So it was sort of a relief when Otto started asking questions.

He wanted to know how we'd managed to find out where he was. How we'd sunk the boat.

"Nice," he said when we'd finished explaining, and I felt a great flush of pride – I'd just received a "nice" from one of the most notorious criminals in the country.

But then he looked at me and said, "All that for thirty grand?" and all that pride disappeared.

I nodded and said, "Thirty grand's a lot of money."

"I don't buy that," he said.

"But I come from a real poor family," I said.

He hooted at that and I didn't blame him.

"Yeah, sure you do," he said. "And that's why you look just like all those other little rich kids who take over my island every vacation."

We crossed a creek, two great wings of water flying up on either side, scrambled up the side of a hill and pulled up at the back of an old shed. From inside came the sounds of pigeons cooing.

"Stay here," said Otto, getting out of the car.

He disappeared behind the shed and I wondered whether I was being set up somehow. But when he returned a minute or so later I had other thoughts, like: *Did he just get a gun he had stashed there?*

I couldn't see any sign of a weapon, however.

"Airfield's on the other side," said Otto. "Reckon it's better to walk it from here."

Just as he finished saying this there was the roar of an exhaust and a car pulled up alongside us.

I turned, expecting to see the blue lights of a police car, the stern faces of police officers.

But instead I was looking at the hot-red of Otto and Zoe's uncle's Monaro, and his rat face. And in the passenger's seat, Mrs. Bander herself, a cigarette clamped between lipsticky lips.

Then the sound of another car, more refined this time, and Cameron Jamison's Ferrari was there too.

He was driving, and there were three other men in the car. Two angry, sodden men, the Mattners. And another not-so-angry, not-so-sodden man.

We all got out at the same time.

A standoff, each group checking the other group out.

I'm pretty sure they came to the same conclusion as I did: that there was an imbalance of power here. Because there were three groups, two guns. Somebody was missing out. Us. Zoe's uncle was

holding one of the guns, a battered shottie, and one of the Mattners was holding the other, an evil-looking AK-47.

Cameron Jamison was the first to speak.

"Shoot them," he said, pointing to our group, the gunless group.

At first, I didn't get it: why would he want to shoot the Zolt, everybody's meal ticket?

But then I did get it: I was going to get shot, I was going to die right here and now.

The man who wasn't a Mattner brought out a video camera and pointed it at us.

There's relief and there's relief, and then there's what I was feeling: relief to the power of plenty.

"We're doing a doco," explained Cameron Jamison. "You can't have too much content."

Once the man who wasn't a Mattner had stopped filming, Cameron Jamison turned his attention to Mrs. Bander and said, "We had a deal."

As soon as he said this, I realized what had happened: Mrs. Bander had shopped her own son! Twice.

She'd turned him in to Hound de Villiers. And she'd done a deal with Cameron Jamison.

Zoe was on to it too.

"Mum!" she said. "How could you?"

"Don't give me that," said Mrs. Bander. "You would've done exactly the same if you were in my shoes."

"As if I'd ever give birth to something like you!" said Zoe.

"Ungrateful brat!" said Mrs. Bander.

Which brought Otto into the argument.

"Leave her alone, Mum!"

As they continued arguing I did a quick analysis of our situation.

A shottie to our left, an AK-47 to our right – we were seriously outgunned.

But what if, somehow, those guns canceled each other out? Then it would be back to a level playing field.

"Where's the money?" said Zoe's uncle, waving the shottie at the Cameron Jamison group.

"Don't you point that thing at me, maggot," said the Mattner with the AK-47.

"Don't you call me that!" said Zoe's uncle.

The Mattner brought the gun up to his shoulder.

"Let's bring this thing right down," said Cameron Jamison, and I have to admit there was something calming, something soothing, about his voice. "There'll be plenty of money for everybody. Of course, you'll have some of the front end. But it's the back end where the serious bucks are made these days. Online. Games."

"I want me money," said Zoe's uncle, the shottie twitchy in his hands.

"Okay, you want your money," said Cameron Jamison, soothing, calming. "Exactly how much do you want?"

I could see the naked greed in Zoe's uncle's eyes.

"Five grand," he said. "No, make that ten grand!"

"That's a lot of money," said Cameron Jamison.

Yeah, sure, I thought. It was probably what he spent on a haircut, on making that hair so super-confident.

"It's my money!" said Zoe's uncle.

"Okay, if you put that gun down I'll get my checkbook from the car."

Zoe's uncle lowered the shottie, and if ever there was an opening, this was it.

"He told me he wasn't going to pay you anything," I said loudly.

"He said that?"

"Yeah, he said a bogan like you deserves nothing."

"A bogan?" he said, pointing the gun at me.

"He called you that, not me," I said, pointing at Cameron Jamison.

"That's rubbish," said Cameron Jamison in that calming voice of his. "I'll just get my checkbook."

Again that shining greed in Zoe's uncle's eyes. "Okay, you get that."

It hadn't worked and I wasn't sure what to do next, how to escalate the situation.

"Uncle Doug, I didn't want to tell you this because I knew how upset you'd be," said Zoe, "but he also said that anybody who drives a crapmobile like yours doesn't deserve a red cent."

The effect was immediate.

"HE CALLED MY CAR A CRAPMOBILE?"

"He sure did," said the Zolt. "Several times."

"So you reckon that Italian machine's any better?" said Zoe's uncle, raising the shottie, squeezing the trigger.

There was an explosion and the windshield of the Ferrari shattered. The Mattner raised his AK-47 and moved towards the Monaro.

"Don't!" said Cameron Jamison, but it was too late.

No empathy. No remorse. And very little brain. The psychopath sprayed the Monaro with bullets, turning it into something that would be just the thing for straining pasta.

Zoe's uncle pulled two more shotgun cartridges out of his pocket, inserted them, moved closer to the Ferrari and gave it both barrels.

The man who wasn't Mattner followed him, filming away: you can never have too much content.

"Let's get out of here," I said to the Zolt and Zoe, my voice low.

The three of us shuffled backwards until we were close enough to make for the car. As soon as he was behind the wheel, Zolt touched the wires, the Mercedes kicking into life. He had it in gear and we were away in no time.

I sunk low in my seat but when there was no sound, no whistling bullets, I snuck a look behind. There were two guns trained on us, a shottie and an AK-47.

But I guess shooting up a car full of kids was very different from shooting up an empty car. Thank God.

We roared away until they were out of sight, but the distant sound of a police siren caused Otto to pull up.

"Let's have a good think about this," he said.

He didn't think for long, maybe about twenty seconds, before he looked at his watch and said, "Next ferry gets in at four forty-seven, right, sis?"

"That's correct."

"And it'll probably be full of cops, but right now I'd say there's only the usual two police cars on the island, right?"

"Right," said Zoe.

"Which means, being cops and all, they'll have one covering the ferry and another one covering the airstrip."

"That sounds pretty cop-like to me," said Zoe.

"You've got VoxMorph on your phone?"

"Of course," said Zoe, sounding a bit insulted: I mean, what idiot doesn't have VoxMorph on their phone?

Otto held out his hand and Zoe passed him her phone.

I watched as he started the VoxMorph app and thumbed a number.

"Yes, hello," he said when somebody answered. "Yes, this is Jack from Jack's Boatshed. One of our boats has just been stolen by Zolton-Bander."

More talking from the other end.

"Yes, of course it's him! You think I don't know what he looks like?"

More talking before Otto hung up.

A minute later and there was the sound of a police siren, a sound that got softer and softer as the police car that was at the airport made for Jack's Boatshed.

Now I was beginning to understand how the Zolt had eluded the cops for so long. And it wasn't, as Cameron Jamison had claimed, because the cops were dumb. Rather, it was because the Zolt was smart.

We continued, finally pulling up at the back of a hangar.

"You're okay to drive this?" Otto said to his sister.

"Sure," Zoe said.

Reverie Island – a place where twelve year olds could drive – sure was a parallel universe to the one I knew.

"But Otto ..." started Zoe.

"This is where we say good-bye, sis," said Otto.

"I want to come."

"It's too risky," he said. "In case you haven't noticed, I haven't exactly nailed a landing yet."

Otto indicated me with a wave of his hand.

"As for the bounty hunter here, it's his call if he wants to come, or not."

The Zolt had stolen four planes, he'd had four crash landings. I'm no mathematician, but I'm pretty sure that was a one hundred percent record.

Surely his luck had to change soon. So basically I had a choice between losing my life or losing my leg to The Debt.

"Well, bounty hunter," said the Zolt, "how much do you want that reward money?"

I looked at Zoe.

She shook her head: *don't go!*

The Zolt had stolen four planes, and he'd had four crash landings.

Surely his luck had to change soon.

Surely he was going to nail a landing this time.

"Let's go," I said.

TRAY TABLES UPRIGHT

We were in the hangar, waiting. It was dark and it smelled of oil. Both of us were wearing overalls we'd found hanging up that suggested we were employees of "Reverie Air Services." Otto had a beanie pulled down low so it covered his forehead. And he had persuaded me to give him my Asics – no pilot wore gum boots, he'd said – so I was the one left wearing the greasy gum boots.

I was so nervous I couldn't stop shaking.

And Otto Zolton-Bander was telling me his life story.

"When I was a kid my old man used to bring me over here," he said. "We'd spend the whole day just watching the planes landing and taking off. He could tell you what sort of plane it was before you could even see it. He was a genius, my old man."

The sound of a plane landing.

"Twin engine," he said. "No good to us."

Then another.

Otto looked out through the gap between the doors.

"Cessna 152," he said. "I wouldn't be seen dead in a thing like that."

I was thinking, *Neither would I.*

"My old man would talk about getting on a jumbo one day and they'd make one of those announcements over the intercom, you know, 'And your pilot today is Captain Otto Zolton-Bander.' And he'd say to the person next to him, 'We're in good hands today, that's my son at the pointy end.'"

I was just about to ask him about his dad, like how he'd died, when another plane landed and again Otto peered outside.

"Perfect," he said. "A Bonanza. You ready, bounty hunter?"

"I'm ready," I said.

"Okay. Let's go."

He slid the door open and stepped out into the fading light of late afternoon.

I kept changing my mind about Otto Zolton-Bander. Mostly I thought he was just another delinquent with a high-pitched voice. But at other times, like now, I was in awe of his daring. Because he just strolled out onto the tarmac in my Asics and nothing in his body language, in his bearing, suggested that he didn't belong there. In fact, he had a sort of swagger, as if this was his rightful place.

"Come on!" he said.

Inspired by his audacity, I followed him out of the cover of the hangar.

The Bonanza had taxied to a stop and two men were getting out. Otto walked straight up to the pilot and said, "Have a smooth run?"

"Smooth as a bucketful of snot," the pilot replied, barely giving Otto a second glance as he handed the keys over.

As the men hurried off, Otto looked back at me and smiled.

"Hop in," he said.

I hesitated. The only planes I'd been in were the type where they insisted you keep your tray table upright on landing. This plane just didn't look big enough, solid enough, to stay in the air. This plane didn't even have tray tables.

"Hurry," he said, indicating the two police 4WDs that had pulled up next to the hangar.

The four forty-seven ferry had obviously arrived.

I hopped in.

Otto turned the ignition, the starter motor whirred, and the prop spun lazily.

"Where's the mixture lever on these things?" he asked, feeling around with his right hand.

The police 4WDs were speeding towards us, sirens blaring, headlights flashing.

“Get out of that plane now!” came a cop voice over a loudspeaker. “You are in violation of federal law. Get out of that plane now!”

“Ah, here it is,” said Otto.

He adjusted something with his hand and the engine kicked in, the cabin filling with noise, the prop whirring.

The 4WDs were almost alongside.

Otto released the parking brake and increased the throttle, the plane gathering speed as we turned onto the runway.

“You are in violation of federal law,” repeated the cop over the loudspeaker.

More throttle and we accelerated down the runway. When the speed reached two hundred and eighty kilometers an hour, he pulled back on the steering wheel, coaxing the plane into the air.

After a minute or so of climbing, he eased off and the plane leveled out.

“Wow, that was amazing!” I yelled over the noise in the cabin.

“Taking off is a cinch,” he said. “It’s my landings that I need to work on.”

As we flew over the strait that separated the island from the mainland and banked south, heading for the Gold Coast, I thought about what Otto had said. Hopefully I’d picked the perfect place for him to execute his first perfect landing.

NAIL THE LANDING

Over the radio, the air traffic controller was freaking out, and I couldn't really blame her: this was the sixth time we'd buzzed the beach. There were people gathered on the sand, waving at us. Obviously the word had gotten out: *Fly Zolt Fly.*

"You need to bring that plane down now!" she said.

Otto hit the off button.

"Panic merchant," he said dismissively.

He banked the plane around and we looped inland.

Below I recognized my school, the busy streets of Chevron Heights, and then Halcyon Grove, like some sort of protoplasm within its cellular walls.

I couldn't help myself.

"That's my house," I said, pointing.

"Seriously?" said the Zolt. "That's some pool you've got there."

I wasn't sure whether I should be proud or embarrassed.

He seemed to think for a while before he said, "Reckon I can drop a coin in it?"

"A coin?" I said.

Otto reached his hand into his pocket, but then he seemed to change his mind and the hand came out again. Empty.

He tapped the fuel gauge lightly with the tip of his index finger.

The needle twitched but settled back down to empty.

"Probably time to land this bird," he said.

"That might be a good idea," I said.

"Got any suggestions?" asked Otto. "One that doesn't involve airports would be good."

"How about over there?" I said, pointing to the rectangle of green to our left. "Ibbotson Reserve."

"There's a strip there?"

"Yeah, they built it during the war. It's pretty rough, but I think it would work."

"You seem to know a lot about it, bounty hunter," said Otto.

I shrugged.

"Ibbotson Reserve it is, then."

First he did a practice run over the park, skimming the trees, buzzing the lake, swooping low over the old landing strip.

"Looks okay," he said as he banked the plane around. "Let's land this baby!"

Now I was nervous again.

"How come landing's so tricky anyway?" I asked as he lined up the strip and decreased the power.

"Flight sim's good, but you know you're just sitting there in a chair."

As if to emphasize his point we hit a patch of turbulence and the plane shuddered violently, the chairs we were sitting in moving all over the place. My guts, too, now seemed to have no fixed position.

As the ground came up to meet us, Otto talked to himself.

Though weirdly enough, his voice seemed to have dropped several octaves.

"Keep the nose level," he kept saying. "Keep the nose level."

I remembered the photo on the net of one of the planes he'd crashed, its nose buried in the earth.

How he had walked away from that mess unharmed I wasn't sure.

But surely his luck has to change. Surely he will nail a landing.

But surely his luck has to change. Surely somebody must die.

The wheels hit the ground, and the Bonanza bounced high into the air.

My guts were in my mouth, my heart was in my gum boots.

This is it, the end of his luck, we're both dead.

Again we hit the ground. Again we bounced.

My heart and my guts changed places.

"Keep the nose level," the Zolt kept saying. "Keep the nose level."

The next time we hit the ground, that's where we stayed, rattling along, the thick grass slowing us down.

My heart and my guts returned to their customary positions and the immense relief I felt needed an immediate outlet.

"Otto, you champion!" I screamed at the top of my lungs. "You champion!"

"Well, I nailed that one," he said proudly.

I could hear sirens wailing in the distance.

I wanted to go, run as fast as I could away from here.

But I couldn't. Though I'd brought the Zolt here I still wasn't sure if I'd repaid the installment. Besides, if I took off it would leave Otto to the trigger-happy cops.

More sirens, and they were getting louder, getting closer, coming from all directions.

We got out of the plane.

Three black motorbikes were coming towards us, engines buzzing like mutant mosquitoes.

On them, bikers in black leathers.

The Debt. They had to be. But how did they find us? How did they know?

As they pulled up next to us, Otto said, "Friends of yours?" and there was a look on his face I hadn't seen before: a little-boy look, as if I'd betrayed him.

I'd caught the Zolt.

I'd done what they asked.

More than they'd asked, because I'd brought him here, to Preacher's Forest.

I shrugged.

The front rider gestured to Otto with a flick of his head: *Get on the back.*

Was he the one who had killed Elliott that day? I wondered.

Otto's eyes were darting everywhere, and I knew exactly what he was doing: sizing up the situation, looking for a way out.

A police car appeared ahead, blue light flashing. And then another one. And another.

Otto, obviously, came to the same conclusion that I did. There was no way out.

He climbed onto the back of the bike.

"But you can't just leave me here!" I said, the sirens getting louder.

The motorbike with Otto took off. The second one followed.

More police cars appeared.

"Please," I said to the remaining rider.

He pointed a thumb at the back of the bike.

I didn't waste any time, I got on.

He dropped the clutch, the motorbike bucked and we were away.

I was astonished at how fast we were going, how skilful the rider was as we flew over the rough terrain.

Ahead was scrub. Once we got in there the police wouldn't be able to follow.

I took a look behind. Somehow, one of the police cars was still gaining on us.

And then it was next to us.

"Stop now!" came the voice over the loudspeaker. "Stop or we will shoot!"

Shoot? Tear gas? Rubber bullets? Surely not real bullets. But whatever they were going to use, it seemed like they had the upper hand. Stopping didn't seem like such a bad option.

It's not what the rider had in mind, though. "Hold on to me," he said.

I didn't hesitate, wrapping my arms around his torso.

"Stop or we will shoot!" said the police.

A glance at my left was enough to confirm that there was now a gun pointing out of the window of the police car.

"You have three seconds to stop," said the cop. "One. Two."

As he said, “Three,” the rider squeezed the brakes and threw the bike into a slide. Now I knew why he’d told me to hold on.

I gripped him tighter.

“Stop or we will shoot!” the police officer continued to shout, but it was an empty threat because we were now enveloped in a cloud of dust.

We came out of the slide, the rider accelerated and we spurted out of the dust and into the scrub. The police cars with their flashing and their wailing couldn’t go any further.

Especially not when the scrub got thicker, more heavily wooded.

We’d caught up to the bike with Otto on the back, and the third bike fell in behind us.

We zapped this way and that between the gum trees. A couple of times I even had to duck to avoid overhanging branches.

I was just thinking that Otto, with his extra height, would have to be even more careful, when Otto, with his extra height, did something extraordinary.

When the bike he was on flew under a branch, he reached up with both arms, grabbed the branch and hoisted himself up.

The Otto-less bike continued on its way, while my bike flew past.

But when I looked back it was to see Otto drop down from the tree, grab a branch that was lying

on the ground and use it, baseball style, on the oncoming third rider.

This motorbike came crashing down, sending the rider rolling over and over across the ground.

But Otto was already wrenching his bike upright, and he was getting on the bike, and he was taking off in the opposite direction.

"Wow!" I said, and why not, it was now the most wow-worthy thing I'd ever seen, far outstripping the wow-worthiness of the Zolt's hideout, like something from a movie that would take days and a squad of stuntmen to shoot. But there was also another feeling: *If he escapes, have I still repaid the installment?*

The rider was on his feet, his arm dangling by his side at a weird angle. The other rider had turned around and was headed in the direction Otto had fled.

My rider stopped.

"Get off," he said.

I didn't need much persuading; I got off.

The rider with the dangling arm took my place on the back.

I watched until the two bikes had disappeared from view before I stepped out of the cumbersome gum boots and got on my own bike, the metaphorical one, the one that had feet instead of wheels.

COLLATERAL DAMAGE

The next day I woke really late, and in my head was this terrible, terrible thought: *You didn't pay the installment!*

But then there was a knock on the door and Dad came in.

"Your grandfather and I have been waiting," he said.

"For what?" I said, but then I remembered. I would be branded after each successful repayment.

"So I repaid it?" I asked.

He nodded.

The question that had formed in my mind – *But how do you know?* – got swept away by a sudden, intense surge of emotion. There was relief – *phew! I did it.* And pride – *wow! I did it!* And fear – *crap! I've got to do this five more times!*

But why was he just standing there? I thought, noticing Dad's bland features. Why didn't he congratulate me or something?

"So, we'll see you at Gus's in half an hour?" he said.

"Do we have to do it today?" I said.

Dad nodded.

"Well, you obviously don't mind a barbecue," I said.

Dad gave me a weird sort of smile and the thought entered my mind: *He actually does like a barbecue.*

But I gave this thought short shrift: no father could possibly enjoy branding his own son.

"Okay, Dad," I said. "I'll meet you there."

After he'd left the room I surfed through the channels on my TV, my thumb not giving any of them much of a chance.

Yes, I'd paid the installment.

But Tristan was in a coma.

Imogen wasn't talking to me.

And I was about to enter the hurt locker again.

What was that phrase that they used all the time when there was a war on? Collateral damage, that was it.

Damage that is incidental to the intended outcome.

Fox News was getting all excited. Breaking news! Breaking news! Breaking news!

A tsunami? I wondered.

Another 9/11?

No, a light plane believed to have been stolen by Otto Zolton-Bander had crashed in the outback. A witness to the crash, an opal miner, said that it was impossible that anybody could have survived such an impact.

A punch in the guts.

Nothing Tristan had done could come close to the feeling I felt right then. Otto Zolton-Bander dead. The Zolt, gone.

Damage that is incidental to the intended outcome.

Well, if this collateral damage continued at its present rate, by the time I'd paid off the sixth installment, my life would be so collaterally damaged it wouldn't be worth living.

Now private investigator Hound de Villiers, the only man to have successfully tracked Otto Zolton-Bander down, was talking.

"If you live by the sword ..." he said, his face huge and craggy on the plasma, but that's all I let him say before I turned the TV off.

It was time for me to go get branded.

Ω Ω Ω

Don't flinch, I told myself as the brand came closer and closer, the letter *P* at its tip glowing incandescently.

But when hairs started singeing I couldn't help it: I drew back slightly.

"For Pete's sake, stay still," said Dad, and again that crazy thought: *He's actually enjoying this*.

Over his shoulder I could see Gus, his eyes wet with tears.

"You're just making it worse on yourself," said Dad.

The crazy thought, like before, disappeared. He, like me, just wanted to get it over and done with.

"Okay," I said, tensing my leg, screwing my eyes shut.

Heat, getting closer and closer, the pain, even worse than the first time, and then the nauseating smell of seared flesh.

One, two, three seconds and the brand was gone.

A low, rumbling sound.

And it took me a while to dissociate this from the other sensations – the pain, the smell – and realize that it was coming from above the house.

"What's that?" I said.

"Some idiot flying too low," said Gus.

Some idiot?

I pulled up my shorts and started for the door.

"Steady," said Dad.

But I kept going, ignoring the pain from my scorched thigh.

Through the kitchen, through the front door and

onto the lawn.

It had to be, I thought.

But how could I be sure?

And then I remembered what he'd said about dropping a coin in my pool.

I ran, the pain from the brand flaring white-hot, across Gus's lawn, across our lawn.

Not breaking step, I tossed my iPhone on a deck chair and dived into the pool, spreading water with both hands.

And there, on the bottom, was a large gold coin.

On it was an eagle, with the words *United States of America Twenty Dollars* above, and *In God We Trust* below.

But it was like no other coin I'd ever seen – the eagle was almost lifelike, as if it was struggling to free itself from the coin's lustrous surface.

I grabbed the coin and surfaced.

There, on the western horizon, I could just make out a small plane, wobbling towards the sun.

I watched until it disappeared from view.

THE
DEBT

THE DEBT
INSTALLMENT TWO
PHILLIP GWYNNE
TURN OFF THE LIGHTS

THE DEBT
INSTALLMENT FOUR
PHILLIP GWYNNE
FETCH THE TREASURE HUNTER

THE DEBT
INSTALLMENT SIX
PHILLIP GWYNNE
TAKE A LIFE
LESSON SIX: HE THAT DIES, PAYS ALL DEBTS

THE DEBT
INSTALLMENT ONE
PHILLIP GWYNNE
CATCH THE ZOLT
LESSON ONE: DON'T MESS WITH THE DENT

THE DEBT
INSTALLMENT THREE
PHILLIP GWYNNE
BRING BACK CERBERUS
LESSON THREE: YOU NEVER KNOW WHO'S LISTENING

THE DEBT
INSTALLMENT FIVE
PHILLIP GWYNNE
YAMASHITA'S GOLD
LESSON FIVE: ALL THAT GLITTERS ISN'T GOLD